A Totally Free Man

***

JOHN KRICH

A FIRESIDE BOOK
Published by Simon & Schuster, Inc.
NEW YORK LONDON TORONTO SYDNEY TOKYO

First Fireside Edition, 1988

Published by Simon & Schuster, Inc.
Rockefeller Center
1230 Avenue of Americas
New York, NY 10020

Published by arrangement with Creative Arts Book Co.

FIRESIDE and colophon are registered trademarks of
Simon & Schuster, Inc.

Designed by George Mattingly

Manufactured in the United States of America

10 9 8 7 6 5 4 3 2 1 Pbk.

Library of Congress Cataloging in Publication Data

Krich, John, date.
    A totally free man.

    "A Fireside Book."
    1. Castro, Fidel, 1927–   —Fiction.
    2. Cuba—History—1959–   —Fiction. I. Title.
PS3561.R475T6 1988 813.54   87-26446

ISBN 0-671-64869-1 Pbk.

Acknowledgments

Writing someone else's autobiography can be less complicated than writing one's own. It can even be less fictional. Where nothing is wholly true, nothing need be wholly false.

Anyone familiar with the limited material on Cuba available in the United States will recognize that a major source of inspiration for my portrait of Castro was Lee Lockwood's revealing *Castro's Cuba, Cuba's Fidel*. Other books which proved especially useful to me were Jules Dubois' *Fidel Castro*, Hugh Thomas' *Cuba*, Ernesto Cardenal's *In Cuba*, Che Guevara's *Reminiscences Of The Cuban Revolutionary War*, Jean-Paul Sartre's *Sartre On Cuba* and *Revolutionary Struggle: The Selected Works of Fidel Castro*, Volume One, Bonachea and Valdés, eds.

Strangely enough, I would never have chosen to undertake this project were it not for the example of an author and a book whose perspective could not be farther from my own: Alexander Solzhenitsyn and his *Lenin In Zurich*.

I would like to express my gratitude to my editor, Thomas Farber, for his discretion and bilingualisms; to Liza Redding, Aron Krich and Toby Cole for the patience that extends beyond the professional.

I was also sustained in my work by the financial support of the National Endowment for the Arts, to whom grateful acknowledgment is made.

Finally, I salute the gallant people of Cuba—in particular, Conchita Pérez, tour guide and dialectician, Raúl and Flipper, bus drivers *par excellence.*

For Ben and Anne,
benefactors

A Totally Free Man

"WALTERS: Do you have a house where you live? No one seems to know where it is.

CASTRO: Yes, of course and I even have a bed where I sleep.

WALTERS: Are you married?

CASTRO: What marriage do you mean, what do you call marriage?

WALTERS: What do I call marriage?

CASTRO: I am not married in the bourgeois sense.

WALTERS: Wait, wait, many of your people, your brother is married in a bourgeois way. You were married in a bourgeois way, you have a son.

CASTRO: Yes, I married once.

WALTERS: And you are divorced. Many people in this country are married. You considered them all bourgeois people?

CASTRO: No, no. Well, there are many interpretations of all this. That is, there are different kinds of marriage. There is no longer the girl who became educated to marry a millionaire. There are differences. But I am going to ask a question.

WALTERS: Why not give an answer?

CASTRO: What is the importance of my being married or not and who cares? These are my problems. They do not belong to international opinion, they belong to me. I can tell you the following: I'm a man that is totally free, that owns my own life. The rest is detail, untranscendental details that have nothing to do with the Revolution nor politics."

—Fidel Castro,
interview with
Barbara Walters, 1977

SIDE
A

Look! It goes, and without the least heave-ho from me. The tape coils, strangling itself. The needles are alert in synchronized twitching. So where is the microphone? Hidden, discreet. A spy—with a memory undistracted by ideology. This little box waits for a harvest of secrets. Let it wait.

Celia, what made you leave me such an inquisitive device? Even in death, your loyalty is a betrayal. Why did you insist on showing me all the right buttons to push?

"Remember, Comandante, you are not addressing an adoring mob of *macheteros*. You must stop talking when one spool is empty, and turn over the cassette . . . ."

Yes, yes, my pet. My dearest of pests. You were right to suspect that I would try to engineer just such a happy accident. Surely I can find a way to outrace this motor in its efforts to catch me.

Yet I made you a promise, and you did your best to hold me to it. Whenever you were besieged with requests for street lights, better hog feed, or new flavors of ice cream, you'd tell the nation they'd get all those things "when Fidel writes his autobiography." No matter how many times we changed the phone number, everyone in Havana seemed to know how to reach that Moorish gazebo left us by Doctor Sánchez, your considerate pappa. A curious place to run a people's government! It was meant to be a cozy love nest for two civil servants—and that's what everyone thought it was. While you fended off callers, lying so unconvincingly about my whereabouts, I'd be reading on the sofa in my undershorts, trapped in the coal mines of Zola's *Germinal*, waving the world away with the hand that held my cigar, hanging a sheet of smoke between us.

"You will get everything you want when Fidel gives us his autobiography . . . ."

She could just as well have said, "When the tobacco stops growing . . ."! But it's too late for me to admit that the people can't have everything, or that Celia can't have what little she wanted. And I'm far past resisting so compliant an audience. Chelita, you know I like to have the last word: a bad habit for a good socialist, for a devout worshipper of the ongoing, of men and institutions "in process." You know better than anyone that I must find inexhaustible listeners, an endless colloquy to get me through the night.

Still, I'd rather you were here to humor me. I don't want to be caught lecturing a stand-in, preaching to this stenographic angel. Now that you've left me unattended, what's to prevent me from putting the boot to this uninvited eavesdropper? Remember what I did to Batista's treasured grandfather clock, to that palace gift from the former King of Silesia? How I heaved it over when I heard that Khrushchev had put his missiles back in his pocket and turned his toy ships around like a good little boy? I have no patience with retreat. And I've even less tolerance for immutable objects, for this neutral inanimacy that hems us all in. I like to show that anything in my range can be transformed. Sometimes, this entails a little petty destruction. But who reported my attack on that defenseless antique? There was no mechanical ear present to capture my unstatesmanlike language or the sound of the watchsprings uncoiling. No one was supposed to witness that unflattering expression of Third World futility.

In regard to such moments, the factual requires a little fine-tuning, an adjustment of levels, a balance of left and right channels. In response to certain controversies, I am obliged to orchestrate, even obfuscate.

"Is it true you once organized a strike of *guajiros* against your own father? Did you threaten to burn down your house if he did not send you to school? And could you have swum across the shark-infested Bay of Nipe with a rifle on your back? How many men did you kill when you were just another university hoodlum? Why is it whispered that you spent the last funds for the *Granma* expedition on a Mexican whore? When, precisely, did you become a true Communist, or are you one yet? And what about your miraculous escapes from assassination? What about the most life-giving escape of all, the escape from your past?"

Suffice it to say, *chico*, I did not spring from the womb in green khaki diapers with a cigar in my mouth and a premature brown beard! Babies are born nonpartisan in the class war. They are not red or white, but quite pink. Nobody comes to the struggle fully formed. Every man is caught in the act of becoming. There's no shame in that. It would be immodest for me to feel chagrin at baring to the world that prisoner of style who was me: the pencil-thin mustache, the thinner black tie, the thick skin to match.

Yet I do feel chagrined. I am one of those animals who likes to cover his tracks.

Besides, certain confusions can be of lasting value to the *guerrillero*. What would have happened if we had allowed Herbert Matthews of *The New York Times* to see how few of us there were in the mountains? So we marched the same men in front of him enough times that they began to look like fresh reinforcements. We told the reporter that I was coming to meet him from a second headquarters when I was merely hiding behind the next rock. Were these lies really? Were they sins, in terms of the old Catholic scorecard or our new, stricter morality? They gave credibility to our cause and sped its triumph.

In the *sierra*, I would also show myself in a peasant village to provoke an attack from government patrols. I'd swagger and act out a crude caricature of a fictitious "Major González," only to make the revelation of my identity more dramatic. Yes, I enjoyed the spotlight then, though my stage was a street of palm leaf shacks. On this tape, too, I might draw you in with mock drama, then demolish you. Storytelling is very much like an ambush. It can be lethal when the story is true.

Of course, the tallest tale is the Revolution itself. Call it a brag that got backed up, to the surprise of all, especially the braggarts. But there are times to face the music, just as there are times to play it. I could have faked the production figures when we failed to achieve the Ten Million Ton Harvest. I should not have announced to all Cuba that our invasion from Mexico would come in 1956. Both times, my top cadre prayed I would choke on my overused tongue. They called me "the gossiping midwife of the Americas." My brother Raúl, for one, swore that I could not recognize a state secret when I saw one. He was right; but so was I.

4

What better way is there to guard secrets than to not have any at all? It was Che Guevara—and the Jesuit priests, my first ideologues—who taught me that truth is much more disarming than guile. In the mountains, this disarmament took on its literal sense. During the worst days of our campaign, when we would have sold our mothers for a couple of plantains, Che reminded us that the enemy would hand over their guns only if we could resist false promises. Che told me: "Bribery is not the way to win over the masses, and the truth is never a bribe." It was Che who first spoke of the transcendent sustenance to be taken from the knowledge that the most severe attacks on our movement, the harshest critiques of our work, would come from ourselves.

Then why do I need more courage to begin this chore? What makes this peculiar shipment of goods so tough to deliver? I have always been dependable, haven't I? I've provided, even if the provisions had to be rationed. I've lived up to the title of *el caballo*, a sturdy mount for the Cuban peasantry to ride. I still answer to El Jefe, Comandante, the good Dr. C. And how does the Yankee dossier read? "Sometimes known as the bearded strongman, the Caribbean jackal, the Soviet Union's best softball pitcher. Military alias Alejandro, or Alex, or Alexander the Great." No man has been given so many names yet been stuck with only one. Fi-del, Fi-del. I am *fidéle* to Fidel.

Who else would be pressing on at this hour of the night? Why can't I lock step to sleep like the rest of the camp? Like the rest of the world? It was in the mountains that I developed this habit. Evading capture, I learned that daylight is good only for the consolidation of position, that darkness is the time one can make a real advance.

When I close my eyes, even momentarily, I picture Johannesburg, Los Angeles, Abu Dhabi. I can't help visualizing all the places where our enemies are busy, and I ask myself, "Why should we lose a moment? How can we afford to cram our fight into a schedule?" I think of the millions of lives being led for private gain, millions plodding through personal agendas, and I want to do something to strengthen and fortify the collective way, the other way. All those grasping masses make me feel dizzy but they don't make me drowsy. I can't give in to my singular needs as they have given in to theirs. I resist the built-in selfishness of being.

I will not go to my bedroom tonight. I don't have much business to carry out in a bedroom, and I never have. Though I come to my beloved Isle of Pines for a rest, it is here, in retreat, that I cannot rest. On this island within an island, I sense most acutely that all our accomplishments are just that: an island within an island.

So, in this crazy backwater, the leader stands watch and the sentries sleep comfortably! Of course, I could wake them for a round of dominoes. My favorite game, where each move leads inexorably to the next. The main qualification required of my guards is an aptitude for playing dominoes at midnight and for discussing international relations while in a doze. Also, they have to move quickly to keep up with me.

This afternoon, I hauled in a splendid skindiving catch: two hundred pounds. I didn't tell anyone I felt faint when I surfaced. I simply needed a good supper, some *arroz con pollo*, Bulgarian yogurt, *chow mein*. Now I've regained my energies. I'm ready to throw the ball for my exhausted German shepherd. "Up, up, Guardian!" Like my Praetorian Guard, he doesn't hear me. Good thing I've got a pistol on my hip. I'd love to fire it, so I could startle them all. I'd like to test my aim. It's been too long since I was tested. Instead, I'll wind up pacing my cage, sliding across the cool patio tiles in my stocking feet, further wrinkling

6

my khaki pajamas. What prank can I pull on the dormitory tonight? This tape, perhaps.

Now I've started. Almost. Let the batteries run while I reach into the drawer for a tin of hard candies and another box of *Montecristo A's.*

PAUSE: THE EXPLANATION OF THE SELF IS TO BE FOUND IN THE OTHERS

If I'm stocking up on cigars, I may actually be getting serious about this task. But what, exactly, is the task? How can I speak about a personal life when I do not believe there is such a thing as personal life? That is the great error of bourgeois culture: always beginning and ending with the individual. In our dying epoch's novels, or at the cinema, the lovers and villians spring from nowhere, are marionettes without strings. I say: show the strings! In real life, does anything begin without sources in other beings, in prior life? Capitalist political science—what I've read of it recently—should be classified as fairy tale. The Cuban Revolution was made because enough Cubans needed for it to be made, not because my father beat me or my mother took me too soon away from the breast. This is a popular game among philistines. I ought not yield to it with gruesome details of my development. I am not one of those given over to fanciful interpretations of the human soul's murky depths, or the reading of tarot cards and astrological charts, or the divination of some untapped essence. None of these are needed to render obvious the acts of a single man, even the most exceptional man. The explanation of the self is to be found in the others.

Truth is the true pursuit of the group. From the richness of nutrients in *la leche maternal* to the quality of lumber for our coffin, we are defined in strictly relative terms. We possess or we are possessed. We have or we have not. (Forgive me, Ernesto Hemingway!) We find his-

7

tory or history leaves us behind. That is why, though I've been called a secretive man, a "mystery man," I have sought to lead the most public of lives. I try to be the last one to find out what I really think or feel, and hopefully I find it out in the midst of a crowd. The important events in a life should be shared events, communal acts. In this I believe I've succeeded all too well.

Look at this room that is my home as much as any other: I'm perfectly content that some Yankee millionaire built it, made sure of the quality of the stucco, took pride in the detailed lead work around the windows. It's not the luxury I like; I prefer the gaps, the faded paint, the unfilled holes left by the luxury that's been removed. My contribution to this imperialist edifice we inhabit has been to make it as bare as I would hope to be. Where a chandelier once swung, I've installed one naked bulb that dims in cycles as our faulty generator loses ground on the night. Around the solid oak table left by the North Americans, I've placed sixteen flimsy metal chairs, garden furniture from our new plant in Las Villas. The chairs don't matter but the men who sit in them do. I draw comfort from knowing these seats will soon be filled by my cadre, my tribe. I would feel more at ease if this were a tent! The only advantage to these solid walls is that we can display the latest poster. This one reads, "WHAT WE WERE IN OUR HOURS OF MORTAL DANGER, LET US ALSO BE IN PRODUCTION." Very fine. My sentiments exactly, though I can't cite the speech. But what do I produce? How do I know when I've met my quota?

I can hardly be called typical, though I'd like to know how it feels. I am always leveling myself out, redistributing my psychic wealth. And I want everyone to measure how much I give to my compatriots, how much I'm given in return. I pity the man or woman who is only capable of a

8

private passion that is kept in a cage like a pet. What kind of existence is it when all that is good and true about a person is revealed behind a locked door? Or saved for exposure to one's "darling" at obscure hours like this? My passion may be misdirected, or overbearing, but it does not skimp on targets. I woo the whole globe. I court my sweetheart with an army. I speak my lover's verses in the *Plaza de Revolución*.

I have always been able to leave my mark because I believe that this mark is all there is to me. What counts is the imprint, not the instrument that left it.

Why, then, must there be such universal inspection of the individual, of his individual gifts, individual failings, individual course? There must be more to it than short-sighted egoism or capitalist atomization. I suppose that life offers us just too much uniqueness. Though we may arrive in quintuplets, we are born alone (aided by the labor of at least one male and one female). Though we may exit in the midst of mass annihilation, we die alone (often aided by our own best efforts). Even the greatest collectivist dies alone. Even Che! That internationalist dropout, who taught so much, held his last class in a one-room schoolhouse, wounded and strapped to a study table, his back to the ink-well. Taunted by drunken lackeys too cowardly to finish the job, he ordered his captors to shoot. He wanted to put *them* out of their misery. Finally, they sprayed him with machine-gun fire from the waist down, so that he would appear to have been killed in battle, thus prolonging his lesson.

Were Che's final thoughts the same as those of the dying prospector in his favorite Jack London tale? Was he taking roll call of the Bolivian children who would have to return to that classroom, or of his own children, for whom he asked no special favors? Was he wondering about me, remembering how I had refused to launch the leaky *Granma* without him? How I postponed our invasion and reduced its element of surprise all because he was stuck in a Mexican jail? Did he blame my foolhardy loyalty for having started him on his fatal course? Did he curse me for being too demanding, for preaching an invincibility that required too many casualties? Was he picturing me at some dreary construction site, inspecting the foundations of tomorrow? Did he begrudge me my job of survival? Might he have imagined that I was about to rescue him one last time? Or was he content not to be rescued? I do not know what he was thinking but I am absolutely certain he was not thinking of himself.

Yet Che was finished, he was finite like the rest. For his sake, for your sake, Celia, for all those who have gone down to remind us that living is for the lucky, I will try to exorcize this individualist demon once and forever. I will do it by means of a tactical retreat, a temporary capitulation. It does me no good to keep quiet, it's too late to cultivate anonymity. The more I refrain from scratching this itch called personality, the more world opinion suspects that I possess grave, incriminating depths. My very denial, and the intensity of my resistance, merely propagates the myth of the primacy of single meanings. The press, especially the imperialist press, keeps asking, "What is Fidel trying to hide? What kink can we find in his straight and exemplary path?"

All the mud hens are digging for dirt. "What are the toilet habits of his Holiness? Who wipes up what He leaves behind?" I understand the source of these questions. Back in Jesuit school, it was the most constant hope of the pupils to catch a priest with a hard-on. And if we Communists have made a new religion, with new saints, then we deserve what defilement we get. So it is gleefully whispered,

"Ho Chi Minh waited tables in Paris... Trotsky ate New York delicatessen while the Winter Palace was seized... Chairman Mao was a third-rate librarian... And Fidel? He was a *croupier* in a Mafia casino... Didn't you know? He was an extra in a Xavier Cugat movie... He failed to impress a scout from the St. Louis Browns."

Without knowing it, I've surely encouraged such whispers. I don't bother with denials because I'm amused by the masses' commendable attempts to make me "one of them." Since boyhood, I've engaged in such demystification of authority. And if authority usually rests on a claim of infallibility, I've tried to see that my authority flows from, or is excused by, an eager admission of human faults. But that doesn't mean I've got to tell all. The most forbidden topics are not necessarily the most germane. Always, they want to look in your pants to find "the real man." I tell you, *chico:* there are other places to look.

PAUSE: THE OLD MAN INSIDE THE NEW MAN

With such disclaimers aside, I am nearly ready to begin. A few sentences down the road, warnings posted, and I am no longer an unwilling traveler. If I was your hostage, Celia, I have now been taken hostage by words. And words are more than those locations where the abstract meets the concrete. They are action without action, moving us closer to our purpose without our having to move. Words are also a medicine with no side effects: the most ready tonic for a nation's morale, for lovers' doubts, for the belly-ache of ambivalence. Once the world before us is parceled out in words, we can move our frustrations about like so much warehouse cargo.

I remember the first time I understood all that words could do. It was the summer after I was forcibly discharged from my "religious training." That would make

11

me eleven, or twelve. It seemed I had lived a lifetime already, first with my stingy cousins in Santiago, then in that horrid boarding school. The house specialities were the torture of the mind in the classroom, accomplished by monotony and short leather batons, and the torture of the spirit in the chapel, through hypocrisy and sexual denial. The order was LaSalle, but they could have been called Spartan. I did not complain about the discipline—at least not in front of my mates—but I hollered when it wasn't applied equally. In the dining halls—medieval places, all mildew and dark oak—I had seen that my brothers and I were served pork while the scholarship students got peppers. I began circulating a petition in protest of this injustice and the general quality of the meals. A priest caught me in mid-conspiracy, at lunchtime.

"And what is all this? How did you gather all these signatures, with your fist?"

"It was easy. Look, this loaf has mold on it . . . ."

"And did the Hebrews complain about the loaves made by Christ?"

"Those loaves were made for the poor!"

The fellow soon lost his Christian temper and threatened to make sure I got to sample the food in the Cuban militia. I responded by shoving the moldy bread in his face. I left that school as a hero.

Back home on my father's *finca*, I continued to get into mischief. Raúl and I went on frequent hunts in the Mayarí Pine Grove, accompanied by some hounds and Ignacio, the old retainer who carried our rifles. Climbing above Oriente's swampy grid, above the ten thousand acres of cane and cattle and lumber that might one day be ours, Raúl and I roamed like predators. Our prey was an end to dependence on all that was below. Where the *sierra* rose from the *llano*, there rose our expectations.

Goodbye to tobacco and citrus and the heat on our necks! *Adiós*, ten thousand phyla of palm! We sought the coniferous. We sniffed for that scent of pine, which pierces this refuge where I now sit, piercing me with a nostalgia for escape. Each time we rose with the altitude, Raúl and I reveled in the discovery of a temperate world, of a fertility that encouraged hope instead of smothering it. We searched for the high ground that shelters all ideals.

Of course, that's not the reason two little boys determined, on one particular occasion, to run away from home. We had often left school outings together, hiding in the bushes for an hour or two to make the rest of our class wait for us. Those escapades were simple dares and so was this one. That is why it was helpful to have Raúl around, why it's always been helpful. Everyone needs a goad. Everyone needs someone who will follow their orders. Probably we ran also because we were not very good with the rifles. We did not relish being "not very good" at anything. So I whispered the right words to my baby *hermano*—was it Martí's definition of mountain climbing as "the manly profession"?—and we were off. Like wild beasts, unleashed from the obsequious Ignacio, just two wild beasts: padding through the underbrush, dodging the thin and nearly leafless hardwoods, sweeping the ribbons of vines from our eyes and tearing the thorny *mamoncillos* from our ankles, feeling the moist earth give beneath the steady demands of our flight.

"*Oiga!* Raúlito! Little devils!" Ignacio was desperate. My seven-year-old brother pitied our keeper. He wanted to turn back and he cried. That was when I started with the words. "Afraid? How do you know what you can do until you do it?" When mere persuasion didn't move him, I quieted Raúl with promises of a warm fire, roasted wild pig, and for sweets, the offerings of this part-jungle, part-tundra where we roamed. We would have our fill of custard apples and prickly pears, strangler figs and pawpaws. In reality, all I could scrounge for my brother was a boulder behind which to hide from the winds at the top of the ridge. For his loyalty, I gave him an early darkness he'd never known, a dinner of acorns and wild orchids. We were lucky not to be poisoned. In place of the fire that somehow would not come from my furious rubbing of stones, I stood on a tree stump and struck a pose I had seen in my first history texts. I gave my first address.

How did it go? "Friends, Romans, hosts of the forest . . . this is Fidel Castro Ruz, son of Angel Castro and Lina Ruz González, proprietors of Las Manacas. I ask your attention and indulgence. I implore you as a humble servant. My brother and I mean harm to no one, man or beast. Our dogs and weapons are down below, left behind with those who might do injury to you, back among those who build railroads and fight wars and go at each other with *machetes.* We have fled that life just as you have fled it. We have wandered astray just as you have. We are hungry just as you are. We face the night just as you do. Therefore, pass on without fear! Pass and leave us be! We are friends who bring comfort and warning. So listen carefully, Cuban deer. Run swiftly! Trust no man! Stop only where you cannot be seen. Wild rodents, be mobile! Dig tunnels, be patient, sharpen your teeth, strike without warning. Then vanish! Resources are few. We must use them to best advantage. Animal armies, march forward with cunning. Eat only when you must. Rest only when you must. Be relentless, be forthright, and survive! . . . I salute you!"

Raúl gave *ovaciónes.* His clapping warmed him as my words had warmed me. We made it through our first night on the mountaintop. Just as I made it through other nights, and will make it through this one, huddled by the campfire of my pretty phrases. But I won't have to descend from the heights—never again—to return dirty and soaked with forest dew, forced to make amends with the many authorities that tyrannize children. That next morning, if I'm not inventing all of this, my brother and I climbed down the wrong side of the big hill and stumbled into a *campesino* village, begging for our breakfast. But the first peasant we saw was so imposing that I did not want him to think we were lost. Approaching him as he squatted on the steps of his hut, facing a suspicion shaded by the brim of his straw hat, I explained, "We're assistants of Castro. We've been taking a survey."

"A survey? And did you find you have enough land?"

"Quite enough, thank you."

"Then why is it you have nothing to eat?"

The peasant invited us to share some plantains and our first chew of *fou-fou*, that bland staple we would one day appreciate with a guerrilla appetite. Delicious stuff, packed with vitamins. I'd love some right now!

For the first time, we sat on the mud floor of a thatched *bohío*. I remember the stench of dried urine. I remember an ageless, encrusted cooking pot. I remember my realization that the heaps of scattered straw were beds for men, not their animals. I am ashamed to say that I don't remember the face or the name of our host. Conditions are so much easier to see than the people in them. Yet I immediately urged the dumbfounded canecutter to join with his cohorts and fashion a set of demands that I would present to my father.

"He would do something if he knew how hungry you are. I'm quite sure he doesn't know about any of this."

I was an imbecile, but an imbecile on the right side. Anyway, I was eager to recover quickly from my poor showing in the Pine Grove. I believe that I helped the pea-

15

sant word his complaints while he drove us back to Las Manacas in his donkey cart. He was scared to be seen delivering us, so he stopped on the dirt road a half-mile short. I was glad; I wanted my father to think we had walked the whole way. I found nothing imposing about the *hacienda* that we were approaching, the rough facade of our home, so unnaturally white, sitting crookedly on pillars that elevated our living quarters above those of the horses and goats. Raúl had begun to whimper. He was imagining the welcome we were about to receive. I had no such worries. Instead of offering insincere contrition for our escapade, I could now greet my father with a barrage of grievances: increase the ration of beans and sugar, send to the city for a doctor . . . .

"Your mother tells me you decided to go camping. That's fine with me. There were two less mouths to feed." My father liked jokes where the punchlines were his power. "I hope you spent an enjoyable night, son number three."

He actually spoke to his children like that, as if by rank! He talked like he was in a Charlie Chan movie. Like a detective, he was always plotting his next move. He had decided to punish Raúl and me by sending for a math tutor to spoil our summer. Later we would take our revenge by swiping a copy of our instructor's figuring book and faking weeks of homework. As for the peasants, my father promised to send them "Christmas packets in July." All I had to do was give him the names of the lucky recipients. I did so eagerly, particularly after my father announced that arrangements had been completed to send me to Havana and the Colegio Belén. I was off to new glory! Not until I returned from a year at the finishing school did I learn that the canecutters had been dispersed and their pitiful shacks burned away.

16

This was all there was to the "strike" I am said to have brought off against my own family. It was a first effort and a first defeat. To act is to do wrong—yet we must act or risk growing more befogged by the social conditions that are always acting upon us. Still, when the July 26 Movement swooped down from the mountains, confiscating *colonias* not unlike my father's, I often thought of those men I betrayed. I was soothed by the song of joy I heard at the *campesinos'* first feast on their masters' cattle. I accepted their trust as forgiveness of my innocent error. Yet I do not mean to imply that some textbook guilt complex made me "take from the rich and give to the poor." If I was an Hispanic Robin Hood, it is because that assignment had to be filled. I detest the condescension of kind works. I reject guilt as an elaborate form of inaction.

Everybody, even the most self-centered brat, has subjective motives for revolt. One doesn't like being spanked, one doesn't like kissing the priest's ring at mass, one doesn't like it that he can't have friends with dark skins. But none of these factors would make a privileged scion risk his privilege or his life. Rather than wait for some magical moment when subjective wishes become objective interests, it is best to lash out. Because once you've lashed, you're in trouble. Then you don't have to bother with trepidation's fine points.

I never had time to examine my motives, not until recently, because I was active right from the start. The connections between head and hands, between a notion and its execution, were as wide in me as Yankee expressways. They have been further distended through years of applied use. I was never a victim of that tropical lethargy which still plagues our people. (I'm sorry, Celia, but they do things too slowly!) I have never been able to wait very long for anything, whether it was a toy battleship for my birthday or a revolution.

17

I suppose all those pediatricians we have trained would tell me that I was not only active, but hyperactive. Strange to think it is considered a disease to have too much life in you, to want so much all at once! I also suffered from the malady of being "accident prone." I would fall off ledges, trip over rocks, stub my toes continually. Then I'd get up and keep going. I welcomed exertion. Whenever I could, I emptied the reservoir of my strength. That was the only way I knew to measure how much life was at the bottom, to find out what hopped and slithered in the muck.

In my first year at the local school in Birán, I could not stay in my seat. I was fidgety, I wanted to be outdoors. Conjugate: *"puedo, puedes, puede. . ."* The teacher kept repeating the same grammar lesson, which I'd memorized for the hundredth time! Also, I felt badly that the other children were so poorly clothed. I was one of the few pupils with shoes. I had to show the others that I could bear hardships, too. So I'd provoke a fight with our matron, throw a paper projectile at her, ask questions she couldn't possibly answer, anything that allowed me to bolt from my desk. One time, as I was running down the front steps of the schoolhouse, I tripped on an empty guava jelly crate. I fell hard, right on the box. One of the nails from the crate stuck in my tongue.

What did my mother say when she saw me? "God is punishing you!"

If she'd been a materialist, she would have asked me why an old crate was lying in front of a school. Today, our socialist teachers may be dull enough to inspire similar flight but at least we've gotten rid of the crates! My mother, in any case, was no materialist and neither was I. However, I had an excuse. I was six years old.

"God tears out the tongues of little boys who talk back."

I believed her and that made me cry all night. Or maybe it was the pain. No, the cruelest part was that I could not eat and I could not speak. Can you imagine a worse place for me to be wounded? Christ was lucky when He was crucified. I would carry stigmata in my mouth. I prayed and trembled all night. I even resolved to keep quiet in class.

However, by morning I saw the incident differently. I concluded that if God had done it, He had been on the wrong side. With my tongue on the mend, I could suggest to myself that God might be just another dictator.

Would you say this indicates I had difficulty accepting authority figures? I've read my Freud, *chico*. I spent a whole month in prison puzzling over a smuggled copy of *Civilization and Its Discontents*. There I found many of my own discontents. And if the imperialists have made a business out of Freud's compassion, if some psychiatrists in *Nueva York* might insist I was locked in a bitter Oedipal struggle, I don't believe that such a great thinker would have endorsed so crude a diagnosis. That's the trouble with having too many disciples! They will trot out the archetype not only when it illuminates but when it obscures. A boy swallows his father, then spits him out to become a man—but I don't view human beings as regurgitating cows. If there is repetition, if there is unceasing imitation, there is also evolution. The Cubans can tell you how far one generation can move. And I must believe there is a distinction between the powers I fought and the powers I imposed.

I did not have an "authority problem." I had an "injustice problem."

Yet in the fight against my parents and their class, I had no choice but to take up their weapons. When I was aggressive and grasping, I was merely following their ex-

19

ample. My father was a clerk who embezzled every acre of land he ever owned. My mother came to our house as a maid, then stole the master from his rightul wife. Given such models, what's remarkable is that I developed the slightest conscience. But the efficiency of my forebears' thievery meant that I could be raised in relative innocence. That's where the dialectic comes in. I became a rebel because I was in a position to insist that society be all it claimed to be: the priest should be holy, the teachers should be wise, the parents should be loving, the crops should be shared, the constitution should be honored, the poor should be gallant in their poverty, or at least be given shoes.

And for the rebel, content in his righteousness, comfortable with his habitual defiance, the cruelest outcome is success. No other result can compromise him so fundamentally, nor force him to perform such psychic somersaults. When we are happily accustomed to banging on iron gates, do we really want to see them open? That's what I got for being too cocksure, too thorough.

My confidence was buttressed by an early access to books—the fuel of all bombast—and by my height. I was a kind of greenhouse Cuban, a mutant, strapping and healthy as, well, as a Yankee. How did their advertisements go? "Helps build strong bodies eight ways . . . ." The Northerners couldn't have known that they were making me in their own image, that they were breeding an adversary their own size. This would have been out of character for the imperialist bullies. And I know the mechanisms of a bully because I was one—how could I help it with my near-gigantism? I was rich, cocky, and mainly huge. In the games I played with my peers, I held all the cards. I had no trouble accepting that this was how it should be, which led to an awful lot of scrapping. Raúl was the only one exempt from my Kid Chocolate punch. He was my one-man gang when I was the terror of the crooked back-alleys of Birán.

I had graduated from pushing bread at priests. I was also quite willing to defend my tormentors, whether or not they requested my services. Returning from a school excursion through the red-light district of Santiago, I charged into a gaggle of prostitutes who were aiming obscene gestures at the Jesuit brothers. The girls spit at me but I kept flailing away. It was an odd sensation, striking the soft targets beneath the flimsy dresses. I was prepared to make war on everything I did not understand.

Luckily, there was sport. Playing stickball between the statues of *conquistadores* in the *plaza* of Birán, or learning *jai alai* on the private courts of my father's more prosperous cronies, I discovered I could utilize my energies to gain instant recognition for my obvious superiority. I was drugged by competition. To be forthright, I must take note of this capitalist addiction. After all, I was a capitalist in training. And I must have learned my lessons well, for I did not like to enter a contest unless I was fairly certain I would win. I was not such a good loser. Grounding into the last out in the ninth inning of a game where an all-Castro team challenged some local boys, I heard our opponents' victory whoops and kept on running, running down the foul line until it was an imaginary line, running through a culvert, then home to my room, where I kept running in my sleep.

If a ball skipped through my legs, I'd immediately point at some pebble on the infield. If I let the baton slip from my sweaty palms in a relay, I'd scream at the boy who made the pass. I was such a boor, I have no idea why I was able to make so many friends. I have to ask myself, "What was wrong with all of them? Why were they so easily cowed?" Being ever-expansive in victory and morose in defeat, I would recoup by forcing my mates to play games of my own invention, games rigged in my favor—like seeing who could memorize the most pages of a textbook. I'd rip them out, one by one, as I pulled ahead. Who knows? Maybe the others just let me win. I learned quickly that winning requires more audacity than talent, that victory is not awarded but taken, that "the best offense is a good defense"—all sorts of sportsman's homilies that I would bring to the larger contest ahead. I could not bring all my trophies. They were too heavy to lug: "Castro, *Campéon*, 100 Meters... F. Castro Ruz, *Ganador*, Basketball, Oriente...."

Now that I'm just another weekend athlete, I root for others. In more ways than one, I am the head *fanático:* running with the piston thighs of Juantorena, throwing my shoulder into Stevenson's right cross. I only wish I could score a knockout each time I enter the political ring! But sports is history compressed; it is a kind of shorthand in which we write the message that the Yankees can be beaten at their own game.

These Yankees wear pin-striped uniforms. For now, the game is baseball. Would Luis Tiant start for the imperialists, with his thousand motions, his pot-bellied connivance? He would not dare try his tricks on fellow Cubans. Poor El Tiante, a renegade from the Red Sox and the red cause! For punishment, his post-game cigar is never a Havana. Still, I would have liked to relieve him. Yes, *chico*, I wanted to play for *Nueva York*. A boy's passions breed contradictory loyalties. Growing up, I had three recurrent wishes: to head a conquering army, to be a lawyer delivering an eloquent summation, and to pitch for the Bronx Bombers in the seventh game of the World Series. Two out of three is no shabby lifetime average.

But it is not true that the course of Latin America was changed for want of a better curveball. It's true I could never master the breaking pitch. As in life, I had a tendency to throw straight down the middle. But I was not destined for *los mejores*. A scout called me once. Appropriately, he wanted to make me a "Giant." He spoke the Spanish they teach in a Berlitz School. "I hear you have a live one, *lanzador.* When can I have a peek at the merchandise?" I agreed to throw for him at the start of the spring term, but by then I had become one of the organizers of a strike to protest the exclusion of blacks from the university squad. We won that struggle and I lost my one chance to go through life with a number sewn on my back. We all have to make sacrifices, eh?

I made up for the loss by leading demonstrations at the ballpark. Those were spirited days! When we knew that the Minister of Internal Security was going to be on hand, we'd pack the stands with students, then charge onto the field with conga drums and banners. While we were out there, a few of us would take our favorite positions. We were going to squeeze all we could out of our foolish protest! So I took the opportunity to test my "high hard one" against visiting big leaguers. I had difficulty taking my full windup in my double-breasted jacket. I toed the rubber with my wing tips. I got resin in the cuffs of my white linen pants. Several years later, I was called to a clandestine meeting of the *Unión Insurreccional Revolucionaria* on that same university diamond. It turned out to be an attempt on my life. The historians have been waiting to hear how I escaped. They would love to find blood on my hands! Let's just say that this was my first tryout in earnest and that I found my curveball just in time.

But I am getting so far ahead of myself! Forgive me. I should stop for a smoke. It is just that I am so much the same throughout this progression. I am always me, unavoidably me. By the time I encountered the guava jelly crate, I had a way of making strangers both curious and afraid. Even when I was dressed for Sundays in a satin shirt, sailor's bow and short pants, I was too hulking to play Fauntleroy. I was more like the plantation's prize-winning livestock. With my shock of brown hair rising like a choppy sea from the reef of my forehead, with my mournfully thick eyebrows, equine nose, dimpled chin and underthroat armored with pale fat, I was something of a walking challenge—and I knew it. When adults saw how soft-spoken I was, how polite and thin-voiced despite the dense eyes, they were quickly won over. I must have observed this dynamic many times, and cultivated a bludgeon of charm.

When charm didn't work, there was always rage. I knew how to throw magnificent tantrums. They could get me a second helping of *congree*, they could get me in and out of various schools. Despite the fact that I was plainly in a better position than the other children I saw, I had the feeling that I was being denied what I really wanted. What I wanted was control. "You're not going to stop me!" But stop me from what? I had to make my choices before I could possibly know what to choose.

At least, this is the way I reconstruct myself. In this attempt, I concede that memory is a selective affair. I accept the censorship inherent in forgetfulness, whether it is practiced by individuals or a movement. I don't holler when the Russians retouch old photographs of the Comintern or eliminate certain documents from their files. Why shouldn't they? And why shouldn't the Cuban Central Committee airbrush me out of existence once they view me as an embarrassing relic instead of a prophet? Each of us does this all the time in our daily lives. We construct the version of the past which gives us maximum strength in the present.

And every account of the past, particularly childhood, must rely largely on the information imparted by others. From the start we look for friendly witnesses to confirm our own assumptions.

Here is what I can remember being told about my first years:

I began pounding on the womb when my mother returned in an ox-cart from buying a new hat at the Yankees' company store in Preston. Getting my first bath, I kicked the midwife until she was bruised. I cried all the time, but my cries turned to speech almost at once. My first words were *luna* and *por qué*. I had no allergies. When I did get the measles, I asked for extreme unction and was given a book about Simon Bolívar. I read that book to Raúl, read him everything, though I knew he could not understand a word. I performed for the politicians and police chiefs when they came to see my father. Afterwards I performed for the maids, doing passable imitations of the batting stance of Joe DiMaggio and the motion of Lefty Gomez, which I knew only from photographs. As an encore, I recited from Homer and Cervantes. I had an intense scientific curiosity. I broke into the kitchen cabinet one night and ate a jar of dried chili pods without complaint. I broke every radio that was given to me and lost so many rubber balls they had to clear new ground to find them. Raúl and I staged great battles with play soldiers, marching metal phalanxes toward Macedonia, in our clubhouse behind sacks of feed in the stable. I would go about calling myself Caesar and Pompey and Alexander the Great, never going inside the house except to eat. I would hide for hours around any convenient corner, awaiting the next victim of my surprises. I soon graduated to stretching invisible string across the busiest passageways. Whether I was in the stable or out in the fields, I would carry a half-dozen composition notebooks. I would fill up those notebooks as fast as I could, even in the dark. I was known to be afraid of the dark, of a demon I called "the thing with no teeth."

And now what I know:

That those chili pods nearly killed me. That I wasn't aware of ever having cried, that I considered myself quiet, so very stoic, no trouble at all. That I loved to sweat and hated to shiver. That I was allergic to all forms of interference. That when I was sick, I got frightened only because I thought I would be buried naked. That I was under the impression all dead people were buried naked, displayed on the shoulders of their friends on the way to the cemetery so that everyone could look them over and find out all that was hidden before it was too late. That I yearned for the sea, but dreaded the swamps. That I was amazed how easily I caught mosquitoes in my grip. That my so-called science amounted to experiments carried out on lizards with my penknife, that I was most curious to see what a frog looked like after I dropped a boulder on it. That I was never afraid of nature, always afraid to be taken away from nature. That I always had a plan. That I learned to read because I did not want to listen. That once, after hitting a home run, I sincerely believed I was perfect. That I wet my bed the first night I spent in Santiago, away from home. That I was really quite timid, and always, on my first day at a new school, I would find a stone on my way and hold it in my fist. That I never wanted the laughter to stop when I performed for my parents, that I hoped it was fond laughter and not the other kind. That I did recite Cervantes, but sometimes I said I was reading Victor Hugo when I was really reading *El Gorrión*, my favorite comic book. That I was no use with a hammer. That I was *número uno* with a slingshot. That I would tell everyone my radios had broken, when really I'd smashed them each time the reception was bad and I could not hear baseball or Jack Benny. That static may have been the cause of my nationalism, growing up with a promise that fades in and out. That I treasured the steely smell of a new Spalding, clean as a bearing, pink as a baby, but I could not help throwing a ball as far as I could. That Raúl was always outmanned in our barnyard battles. That I worshipped Alexander the Great, because the picture books showed him fighting naked except for his shield, which seemed doubly courageous to me, so that twenty years later I took his name. That I also imagined battles taking place inside my morning bowl of oatmeal, troops swimming from island to island through a sea of milk. That I always knew a fake war could not compare with a real one. That, like all children, I was a militarist because I thought I was immortal, and that this later made me a good general. That I played my pranks because I found my elders were honest only when they were shocked. That I was filling those notebooks of mine with lists, lists of everything I saw or felt. That I listed my heroes:

Alejandro
Lefty Gomez
Bonaparte
Bolívar
Hamilton and Burr
Hemingway
F.D.R.
Wyatt Earp
Don Quixote
Donald Duck

That I listed my favorite cooks and dishes:

Conchita, *flan* with cinnamon
Juana, pork stew
Salomé, christians and moors
That I listed favorite subjects at school:
Ancient history
Rhetoric
Gymnasium
And least favorite:
Geometry
The Bible
Study hall
And cities I wanted to see:
Rio and Sparta
Caracas and Baghdad
Barcelona and Camagüey
Cairo
Paris
Of course, *Nueva York*
And colors:
Mauve
Raw Umber
Evergreen
And creatures:
Grizzly bears
Mandrills
Tropical penguins
And changes I wanted to make in Cuba:
Shorter school year
More rivers and lakes
Girls who can play baseball
Snow
Papaya ice cream for my friends
Bombing and desecration of select churches
That I am still making lists, that I am still taking inventory

of a nation. That the lists were my truest companions. That they made me forget my fear of the night.

But why inventory what's vanished? This must be a self-induced delirium, a product of the intoxication that comes from knowing my customary audience is deafened by sleep. In any case, we can erase all of this later. A little Nixonian gap, eh? No, the Cubans do not allow gaps. They cannot bear silence, but insist on a mighty noise! Or is it me that does the insisting? Again, I am obliged to look for the answer in childhood. But please don't think I'm merely following a convention. We all live chin-deep in the past, and revolutionaries, for all their ranting about the glorious future, are more obsessed than anyone with this bad piece of property we all inherit. They know best that the past is the ultimate, the all-pervasive enemy.

We are all of us trapped in a universe of befores and afters. I am well aware that a beginning is only an arbitrary point, that a birth is never immaculate. Though historical materialism tends to foster a linear view of development— each epoch advancing over the last, every great cause proclaiming the distance it has come—we need to see the traffic of our "fellow travelers" by putting a few bends in the course. We ought to view time as a circle. On the first curve of the Cuban circle there was Manuel Céspedes, the original renegade nobleman; on the second curve, Maceo and Gómez, better strategists than me; on another curve, Eddy Chibás, that most eloquent maniac. So many behind me, so many with me, so many ahead of me. If I begin in childhood, it is to find the old man inside the new man, the new man inside the old man. There is nothing else worth going on about at this hour of the night.

PAUSE: NOT EVEN MARX WAS BORN A MARXIST

There must be a reason for all behavior, a clear and evident cause. If we have not found an explanation, that doesn't mean it's not there. I despise everything commonly contained in the category of "human nature"—that cowering before vagueness, that erosion of the rational—which threatens all our efforts toward clarity and debases those few miracles that are really beyond our understanding.

The most ordinary factors make a man exceptional and the most exceptional factors make a man ordinary. The Cuban people are familiar with the sources of my boldness, my oratorical skills, my yen for mammoth cigars. Everyone can add me up. Access to education plus exposure to the peasantry plus proximity to fresh air, multiplied by unusual physical capabilities, equals one crazy young man who did not know how to doubt himself or his country's destiny. Change one variable and poof! There goes Fidel!

Suppose I'd been hatched a few miles to the north, a few hundred miles, suppose I'd been a "true blue" American! I might have been a delinquent in some *barrio*, running the streets in pegged pants, zoot suit and high-top Keds, thwarting all correctional efforts, driving full speed into a brick wall in a stolen Studebaker. A Latin Jimmy Cagney! Or perhaps I would have been the crusading storefront lawyer, rescuing wayward boys from prison, turning "spics" into loyal citizens, dishwashers and porters. You see, I was just an average Cuban. I have no trouble recalling our implanted daydreams.

But the closest Northern analogue to my birthplace would be a cotton plantation. "Down yonder in Dixie," correct? My father, bless his heart, was an eccentric English gentleman, a white's white, ready to die for the Confederacy, with holdings in slaves and magnolias. I didn't approve of the former, so my father packed me off to a military academy in Virginny. But I got my revenge. I ran away to Washington, married a high society belle, was elected to Congress, and finally came home as a lieutenant fighting for the other side. The old homestead was a shambles and so was my daddy. With the help of the freed slaves, and my belle, we worked to rebuild the plantation. Happy ending! *Felicidades!*

I saw such a film once, when the screen wasn't obscured by my classmates tussling in the aisles, at a matinee in Santiago's *Teatro Del Rey*. The film starred Randolph Scott and Claire Trevor. Luckily, the economic blockade has kept us from seeing the updated version of this success story. Cubans have learned the hard way that Hollywood movies are the only locales where one can have principles and also be rich.

As a child, I learned everything the hard way. I took what I wanted, asked permission afterwards. Oh, I asked plenty of questions too. But they were not the usual kind. My rendition of "Why is the sky blue?" was "Why does that man have less than I do?" I got the usual replies. "Because he's lazy." "Because it's God's will." Everything I was told confirmed the fact that the world I'd been placed in was not of my own making. This in itself is a commonplace. What was not so common was that I kept testing the assertions of others, kept prodding. I began cross-examining when I was in the crib. I was looking for one unified motive for the crime known as Cuba. I wanted a verdict in harmony with my own perceptions. In the end, this verdict was Marxism. If I took my time coming to it, I am not alone. After all, not even Marx was born a Marxist. He too must have begun with simple questions.

My first questions had to do with the ironic deformations of colonialism. They were obvious: Christopher Columbus had stumbled on a paradise, but everything had run downhill since 1492. Anyone could see that the paradise was no longer fit for habitation. Anyone, not just me, could see the fertility of the land and the poverty of those who worked it.

My father's *finca* was a front row seat from which I could observe the inequities of the sugar trade. *Azúcar:* the sweet shit, our candy mistress. The Castro lands were worked to feed the *Central Miranda*, a typical Yankee sugar mill with its typically inexhaustible cravings. The cultivation forced upon our soil was not evil merely because the imperialists could purchase the results at artificially low prices. No, this was an adrenal harvest. It entered directly into the bloodstream of our enemies and powered their demonic enterprise. Listen, *chico*, everything is rooted in physicality: the western world's domination of the planet is a matter of caloric imbalance, the hoarding of glucose and sucrose.

What was more American than apple pie, that Yankee tartness sweetened with Cuban sugar? From our brethren nations they got the coffee to wash it down. Overstimulated by our caffeine, they've been gobbling the Third World like a banana split. The real "energy crisis" will come when such appetites can no longer be satisfied! Here again, nature works in our favor: Russian nutritionists tell us that sugar places a fatal strain on any system which depends on it. Yet the Socialist bloc also licks up all they can swallow; we fatten the world impartially.

Does this account for my inordinate hungers? Is that why I have always been in a contest to devour everything in sight before it devours me? Enough! In a minute, I'll have to run to the pantry and correct my own caloric imbalance.

But sugar does not sprout as a delicate powder to be sifted gently with a monogrammed spoon. The cane is like thick, unwashed hair that smothers the pores of our land. Cut the stumps and they grow back for six seasons. Not so well-suited to socialism's earnest toil, it was a perfect crop for the absentee planters, off getting cultured in Paris, gambling their windfalls away at Monte Carlo. All that surplus value, with only the quick work of the *zafra!* And when there was no work, during the *tiempo muerto?* Let the peasants live off berries, let them run out of kerosene! Why keep Cuba lit? There was nothing to see. Just some dancing savages and a few hotheads.

It was a marvelous arrangement, this cycle of under-employment and enforced indolence. I appreciate it all the more now that I've had to construct a new economic order. The trouble began when we pledged that there would be no more "dead time." A full-time job for every-one, everyone who does not shirk—even if that means having six attendants for each public toilet and three operators for each hotel elevator! At the psychiatric hospitals too, we pay a salary to the catatonics who can be roused to make music for the other catatonics. For us, work is heroic and redemptive. This has nothing to do with dogma or the efficient use of resources. It is not a result of that continuing slavery called having-too-little-for-too-many. Cubans have historic incentives for valuing opportunities to apply themselves. They like to go to bed properly tired and wake with a task that needs doing. That is, most Cubans.

There are too many who remember what it was like when we were a kept country. All we had to do then was work on our tans, straighten our hair, polish our nails. Never mind if we skipped a few meals and couldn't write our names! We had to please sugar daddy. Oh, daddy, daddy . . . sugar daddies are not so generous as they seem. They take you in their laps, like Santa Claus. They ask you what you want for Christmas, and before you know it they're sticking it up your ass.

Santa Claus always wore a fake beard. I'm tugging on my beard right now but it isn't coming off. And some of our overgrown children in Miami are moaning because we no longer permit "an old-fashioned Christmas"!

My native Oriente, our frontier, our "wild, wild East," was renowned for its tradition of ingratitude. The legendary recklessness of its bandits and lunatic patriots, the thirst for self-destruction which I soon acquired, was born of the lack of responsibility that comes from being owned. The ground we farmed was owned; the government and its minions were owned; cultural expression was owned; the people's self-worth was in hock.

But I wasn't. I was a first-generation Cuban, like nearly all our furious insurrectionists, present and past. None of us had a chance to get used to life in the pawn shop! The Spanish sentenced the seventeen-year-old José Martí to work in a quarry with chains on his feet; he made those chains his "marriage ring" to Cuba. Like me, the great apostle was the son of a Spaniard who'd left him a legacy of European expectations. Like me, he started out believing that the society in which he was born had some rational order. Like me, he memorized the constitution and its sovereign provisions. Like me, he was a patriot. We were both upstanding citizens of a nation that did not exist.

We were both internationalists too. Such a perspective is easily achieved when your country is continually overrun, when the beloved fatherland is a doormat with palm trees. Cuba was the last Spanish holding to gain independence—but then, as Martí predicted, we found ourselves with a President named Mister Magoon! The U.S. Marines were sent to end strikes in our sugar mills. In the countryside, a day's work belonged to the Yankees. In the city they took our nights too. Everyone dreamed about being American but the Americans didn't need Americans anymore. They required plenty of "good Cubans." A good Cuban was someone who wore a straw hat. A good Cuban jabbered constantly and was uncontrollably emotive. A good Cuban had style and pride and could dance just like "Hector y Veloz." A good Cuban spent his *pesos* on "Made in U.S.A." His ideals were "old world," his underwear "Fruit of the Loom."

I don't entirely blame the Northerners for failing to comprehend the dimensions of the servitude they imposed. Up there in the industrial zone, man stands on his own ground. He is the captain of his own progress. His excesses are in pursuit of that progress and therefore forgivable. If he is estranged from his achievements, if he can't be happy in the world he has made, that too is somehow noble, a commendable response to his unquestioned supremacy. If twentieth-century man chokes to death on his automobile exhaust, he's at least enjoyed the ride. If he pushes the final button, he's at least had the pleasure of designing the button. He may complain about the mess he's made but in his heart he is comforted to know that it is *his* pollution, *his* radiation, *his* moral filth.

This affirmation was built upon what we were denied. We could not destroy Cuba without asking the Yankees' permission. We did not enjoy the fundamental right to make our own garbage, to be fouled by our own wastes. How could we even think to clean up? Above all, we did not possess a future. On what outcome could we bank, for what prospects could we toil? Where was this twentieth century we'd heard so much about? The answer to these questions was revolution. The Revolution was made inevitable because the natural habitat of man is not at the edge of a cliff.

I grew up on that cliff; it made me want to leap. Most people simply learned good balance. Our view was monotonous. Everywhere we looked in my beloved Oriente, across the tops of the silver-fringed palms, we could read an invisible sign: "Property of the United Fruit Company." We called it "La United," and we knew it as *la miseria*.

It's not really so strange that I keep harping on this matter of ownership, I who denounce private property! I came from the proprietary sector and I have proprietary instincts. I am accustomed to walking on ground that bears my name. Such feelings are unavoidable; if they weren't, there would be no reason to oppose the class system! Now all Cuba has become my farm. I can run it without holding the deed. I can requisition every tractor, count each sack of nitrogen fertilizer, plant my experimental hybrids. I can prove my "green thumb." I am the last *latifundista*.

Ironies lurked around my family, too. You see, my father and mother had striven for wealth and respect in a country where wealth was measured in fear and respect was an undiscovered resource. Las Manacas, their idyll, was gained by deceit, maintained by bribery. Their mansion, our home, was built for expropriation. My parents, for all their comforts, lived in suspicion and turmoil—and asked us to be the heirs to their precarious throne. We had a traditional family in that we were preached the gospel of family against all. We needed external proof, and the frequent prod of adversaries, to be a family at all. Between ourselves, in the entrails of our shaky fortress—grandiose archways, white tiles popping from their grout—it was Angel versus Lina versus Juana versus Lidia versus Ramón versus Raúl versus Pedro Emilio versus Angela versus Fidel. Each of us had to learn to hold our own, to rant. We shouted and hollered until the shout became a caress.

"Mouseface! Sour milk! A little girl doesn't need so much dessert!"

"Thugs! I'm a princess! Bow your heads before the princess!"

"Close your lips, your highness!... The Mayor wants me to donate a heifer for the *fiesta*. Why doesn't he take one of my daughters?"

"The richer they get, the more charity they want!"

"Which explains the behavior of that bastard son of yours . . . ."

Which brings me to the fact of my illegitimacy, that most illegitimate fact. Alright, technically I was a bastard—certain governments still consider me one—since the union of my mother and father was sanctioned well after my birth. So what? This sanctioning meant even less to me than the previous lack of it, though both may have made me more combative. In Oriente we did not deal in semantics. No "grey areas." Just black and white, and purple rage in our hearts. Anyway, I was never much of a Catholic, and my father and mother always looked quite enough like a mother and father to me. Not that I am certain every child needs to have a mother and father, except in the genetic sense, where we have no choice. All of this is quite over-rated, I believe. Normality tends to breed only normality, rarely greatness, or better still, goodness. When the people shout, *"Qué bueno!"* That is my faith. That is my Catholicism.

Why did I then try so hard to construct my own family? Why did it take me so long to relinquish the sentimentality I felt for the Castro cartel, for that mouth-feeding unit? I have asked myself many times, "What, concretely, was the source of our intimacy?"

I have concluded that the efficiency of a family can be charted in direct proportion to its faith in the illusion that other families are competing against it. The family is the most basic form of private property: emotional private property. The means of production are the means of re-production. Just think of the surplus value earned by children bred from the inexpensive raw material of sperm and egg! The maintenance of this assembly line of descendants is capitalism's fundamental, and fundamentally unchallenged, premise. No wonder our day care centers and collective nurseries horrify even the most sympathetic liberals! You would think they'd be relieved to know that some individuals begin life without the crippling influence of those all-purpose models, the dread enforcers, mamma and pappa. But these critics of ours have not let go of ancestry's profound conceit, of the pure egoism that pits one furtive copulation's product against the next.

What a heartless waste of time childhood is! Why does it take so long to find out there is nothing to find out? No rules to live by, no sure-fire method for avoiding the pitfalls of our peers. My upbringing was the first phase of a long struggle and the least enjoyable phase at that. I carry no illusions about a golden time when reality could be whatever I wished. Wishes belong to the powerless. Working in the night like a safecracker, a boy's vaunted imagination is merely picking a lock. And I saw locks all around, though I was given an estate and a countryside to roam. No, I have grown up into childhood. I have fought for my "golden time."

Still, it may be true that nobody is capable of a full escape from the hatchery. This would be an ideal and men are not ideal. There are no heroes, just lonely explorers, hacking their way through life's underbrush. From feudalism to capitalism, capitalism to socialism, there can be no "skipping of stages." You can look it up in Lenin. So how can we expect a helpless individual, an unformed boy, to skip stages by breaking his feudal bond to those who gave him life? We are all born as pawns, ready to believe anything, ready to be tricked, the way I was tricked by my father when I tried to arouse his laborers. The standard equipment of the human race is gullibility. Why is it that we are all so appallingly eager to accept what's passed on to us, to live by definitions of good and evil that we ourselves have no part in shaping?

Luckily, time is the ally of all good tidings. Everything that lives is susceptible to rapid and drastic alteration. Take my father and his cruel designs: all gone now, all expropriated by *me*. And with no apologies! If sons were not meant to surpass their fathers, then the earth would not spin but simply flop in space like a sea bass on my harpoon. Poor Angel, *mi padre*. He could grab what he wanted, just like me. He did not hear the word "never," and neither do I. He hated the Yankees even more than I do, for in my hatred there is at least a little bit of envy. He was a Spaniard to his spleen, a Gallego, with the well-known Galician temper, born into the well-known Galician poverty. I'd like to see my ancestral home some day. I've been invited by the many Castros back there, for Castro, they tell me, is the most prevalent name in those Northern hills of the motherland. It is a name of military derivation, I'm proud to say, taken from the ancient word used for Celtic battlements. I've brought over a few of my Castro cousins—Rafaelito the probate, Felipe the goat herd, a taciturn bunch—plied them with rum, lent them jeeps and drivers, provided them with everything except pretty escorts. We don't do that anymore. But I hope they were impressed. Strangely enough, I really wanted them to see the peculiar way in which one of their clan has made good.

The success story began when a rich landowner paid

my father to take his place in the Spanish army. This evasion of service was one luxury my father would seek for his children. Too bad we went out and made our own war! So my father was shipped to Cuba to fight Teddy Roosevelt and his boys. He was not a Yankee hater then—that came after he was out of the line of fire. In fact, he stayed in Oriente so that he could work for United Fruit. In this capacity he found a way to avenge the Spanish defeat. He was a bookkeeper who learned too well how to "adjust" the books. He took his share of everything that passed through his ledger: a little sugar here, some land titles there. What the Yankees confiscated, Angel Castro confiscated. When Spanish soil was stolen, my pappa returned some of it to his own Spanish hands. On moonless nights he would hack new ground from the forest of Mayarí. In the morning, the peasants would wake to find the Castro holdings mysteriously enlarged.

One *hombre* building his fence against the universe: it's preposterous. Sometimes I think class interests are as idiosyncratic as sexual attractions. Why a man seeks a particular woman and why he seeks a particular niche in society are both urges that are incomprehensible to all but the one who pursues them. Why did he need to get rich? He could go a year without changing his shirt. Why did he seek power over our dusty corner of the valley? There was no purpose to that power other than its self-perpetuation. My father did not collect folk art or favor a patron saint. He had no taste, no tradition, and less imagination. He did not even feel secure, but carried a peasant's suspicions always. He finally came to accept the "monsters of the North" as new economic masters, but he would never forgive them for diluting an imaginary Hispanic civility to which he aspired. In his furtive way, he longed for a code of values that might have tempered the New World's barbarity, and his own.

He was indeed a barbarous man. I'm not referring here to his table manners, though his, like mine, were a bit rough. No, I mean that he never developed any sort of morality. He was a great ape whose chosen tree was our *finca*. In my adolescent shame, I began to think of him as the missing link between man and beast, as mentioned in our textbooks, a biological mistake breeding an outcast race. In fact, he was most appealing when he churned through the forest on a tractor, engaged in unlimited ravagement. Once, when I was very small, he had let me drive the tractor while I sat on his lap. I have to admit that I nearly admired him.

I must also give him credit for handing me my first cigar. Probably he was hoping to stunt my growth! It was after an Easter supper that I performed this rite of manhood. I was so proud, imitating my father's sucking and his brief contentment. He used to tell me, "The only thing as good as a cigar is another cigar." He indoctrinated me when I was only ten.

But all parents look normal to their children. To see their flaws is to begin to see one's own. It did not take me long to see that my father was never happy unless he was involved in some project aimed at increasing his earnings. He had to be in charge of every detail, to lay each line of pipe himself, to get in everyone's hair. Does this sound like someone we know? It is not for nothing that I have been accused of *paternalismo*.

Angel Castro, like me, was a presence, a whirlwind, a slob. The floppy pockets of his *guayabera* were always stained with cane juice and wine; his fingernails were dirty and made a nasty sound when he clawed his desktop, casting about for important receipts. At least he was clean-shaven—a trait I've shown no inclination to imitate—but he smelled of a cheap cologne my mother bought by the jug. At Easter, the fragrance of that cologne filled the nave, overpowering the altar boys' incense. His children were the ones who were embarrassed. To us, he seemed to be going bald forever. On special occasions, he would cover his dome with a wide-brimmed planter's hat for purposes of intimidation. This was his major concession to vanity. He went everywhere in his riding puttees.

Actually, we rarely saw him. He had supper with us only when he could find no excuse to be elsewhere. Often he'd show up with a terrible headache and a towel wrapped around his head like a turban. He would scream at us if we dropped a fork or left a bit of sweet potato uneaten. When one of the children got into real trouble, we were sent to his office. It was more like a stucco cell, furnished with a mahogany desk covered by old newspapers and little safes for which he could never find the keys. Often he would sleep by that desk in a white cotton bedroll. He had no use for interior decoration, even less for neatness. He liked to supervise his great works, but at the center of the project, around his tractor, there was emptiness. This is the same vacuum in which I like to move, a cleared field, a space in the rubble, stripped of pretense, which many of my comrades find more imposing than a palace. They know I'm not just playing with symbols when I travel the land with my pup-tent. They fear me because I spring forth without need of a cocoon. They sense that I'm not just accustomed to impermanence, but that I prefer it.

The house my father built was large, too large to be properly tended. It was rustic without charm; before it was old, it was falling apart. You could smell the animals through the floorboards. The foundation was bad. Yet I've gone a step further. I cannot imagine having a home at all, though I've tried, tried mightily to domesticate. Didn't

I, Chelita? I just could never see the sense in a neatly arranged living room where nobody ever lived. Family portraits on the walls: each apartment its own ancestral shrine. Over every quaint stove, the "homemaker" herself, a beloved slave. A million neat living rooms, touching only in that they are so alike; a million shrines, pathetic in their threadbare gaudiness.

Just as I can't feel this longing for a hearth, I can't share in the Cuban weakness for the baroque. Our people insist on making the most of what little they have. Because they once lacked what was basic, they learned to appreciate life's embellishments. Hungry girls danced in *conga* lines with baskets of inedible fruit on their heads. I have tried to be tolerant of this tendency; I'm even a bit envious. Life would assuredly be more pleasant if I were able to find comfort in the stylish execution of irrelevant details. But I am trying to preserve this consolation for our people. I've proposed edicts banning Sovietized names like, "National Foodstuffs Outlet Number Twelve." Let them hang onto their *"Panaderias de los Milagros."*

There will always be *postigos*, those jigsaws our people persist in cutting, our doors within doors within doors. There will always be carnivals, pageantry to pass the warm nights, outfielders who catch line drives behind their backs. There will always be jovial taxi drivers to tell the tourists, "A Cuban lives his true life at the beach." What can we do with that? Build sand castles instead of public housing? There will always be *orquestas* in frilled shirts, tapping out the *charanga*. There will always be slave drums and elaborate valentines, dark-lit clubs. There will always be a midnight show at the Tropicana. An eternal Cuba, and a fleeting Fidel.

National character, like individual character, can be terribly stubborn. But perhaps I'm more like the rest of my countrymen than I'd like to admit. I play my games too. It's just that I prefer to tackle matters directly, without the protection of flourishes and trumpets. So did my old man. He treated his children the same way he treated his farming. He would call for me during breaks in his interminable accounting.

"You were misnamed, son number three. There is not a trace of fidelity in you . . . ."

"I can be loyal, but only to ideas."

"Ideas don't pay your tuition, eh?"

That was a typical exchange. And I'd say something like, "I can't see it that way. I do not have a mirror in my room."

"What? What is it you want from me now?"

"I was speaking figuratively . . . ."

"Then speak Spanish . . . . You are not a spoiled *norte* yet. If you don't behave, you will shine shoes with the mob in Madrid, you will sell brandy at the *plaza de toros* . . . ."

Is there a father in this hemisphere who has not handed this line to his son? Everywhere in the New World, there is the implicit possibility of a return to the Old. History can be reversed, the fathers warn. But the sons know nothing of what was left behind. The threat has no force.

Soon enough, I was doing the threatening. Raúl and I became so unruly that we had a special class created just for us. Not the seventh grade or the eighth grade, but a retrograde Castro grade: offered as a privilege, we knew it to be a preventive isolation. The Jesuits put up with us only because of the potential donations represented by my family. Finally, after we'd smuggled a myna bird into study hall, where it addressed our favorite disciplinarian in language we could not use, my father decided he could no longer subsidize our mayhem. We were summoned to

Las Manacas. Raúl, the crafty one, welcomed this final expulsion from obligation. Like many a teenager, he had romantic notions about "getting an 'A' in life." My attitude appeared more hard-nosed, though it was really prompted by emotional considerations. I would have been lost without teachers to outwit, rules to spurn. Upon our arrival home, a session was convened that resembled the United Nations debate on Palestinian autonomy. I issued the ultimatum: "Either I finish my schooling or I burn down the house!"

Happily, I did not have to carry out my plan. I can just see myself, trembling, gasoline can in hand, about to torch the ancestral home. I only wish I could have been so daring, so detached from false sentiments! My father laughed in my face, laughed and acquiesced. Damn him! Here I was girding myself for a good fight, for that bite of raw involvement called conflict—and he thwarted me again. I think he knew that the worst form of punishment for son number three was "permission granted." I would have free rein when I wanted to prove I could fight my way out of a trap. For all his bluster and obstructionism, my father encouraged me to do what he did not have the nerve to do. When it came to a critical point, he was a pushover. He was just like Batista. And like Batista, he fell of his own weight, relieved to let go of the mess he'd made.

When you start out to make a revolution, you think the transfer of power will be the hard part. But power is there to be grabbed, accessible and easy. It's the bits you take for granted—food on everyone's table, love in everyone's hearts—that turn out to be hard. No wonder I still feel untested, through all the travail. Naturally, I'm not tired out yet. I'll never get tired!

Oh, my parents went through the motions of applying the customary restraints of childrearing. They often said "no" so that we would be disciplined enough to earn the "yes" of success. Today, the Cuban state goes at it quite differently. We say "yes" to our children, we give them all we can afford, so that they may achieve a society in which "no" may be heard. No to greed, no to ambition, no to false pride.

When it came to false pride, my mother was the specialist. She tried to be a thoroughbred but she was just a plow horse. And she always wore blinkers. I would have liked to know how to remove them. For a former servant she had no consciousness of servitude. She had come to my father's house as a laundress, Lina González from Pinar del Río. She was crafty, compact, slightly bow-legged. She could have been called pretty were it not for that horse's nose I inherited. In the days before her red wig and her bifocals, she must have possessed sexual powers. Thank God I never saw them. I had enough problems! I would guess she seduced my father with a display of ruthless confidence. They were certainly a match in self-congratulation.

My mother was tough and openly selfish and quite unlike the forever sacrificing Latin mamma. My mother did not coddle, she pushed. Her children were special and ought to do their best to prove it. She used to declare, "If a Castro cannot do it, no one can."

Like most children, we pretended not to be listening. But we heard.

And we saw her doing everything, from entertaining unctuous politicians to tending prize-winning bougainvillaea to saving *centavos* in a crockery jar. She was thrifty, to put it mildly. She could not get used to spending money because she was not used to having any. Was that why I turned out just the opposite? Why I can never hold to a budget, why the government's in debt now? Clearly, my

46

mother did not teach me the value of money. But she did make sure that if I was spoiled I was never babied, not even as a baby. Thanks to her, I did not become one of those men in our culture who are all chain mail on the outside while they search for a breast to suck.

Tell them, Celia. I did not suck on you. And I know how to cry.

And I know how to talk seriously with a woman because I could talk with my mother. Or at least, she could listen to me as my father never could. In the breakfast room, hand-painted with stenciled rosettes, my mother would crochet while I poured down cup after weak cup of *café con leche*, filling her ear with a schoolboy's philosophy: "You know what I want, Mamma? I would like, just once, for the teachers to sit in our chairs, to squirm there, while each student takes his turn before the blackboard. How can they gain our respect unless they respect us? We only howl because they treat us like a pack of wolves. It's not fair, and it's not a proper view of human nature. Have you read Ortega y Gasset, Mamma? We are not here to deny anything! We are here to confirm everything!"

My mother would mutter back, "All you need is a good woman and you'll settle down. A good woman wouldn't let you keep your room the way you do . . . ."

She had long since given up tidying the sandwiched heaps of dirty socks, notebooks, catchers' mitts that Raúl and I left everywhere. She must have felt she was playing jacks in a hurricane. From her point of view, our politics were just poor housekeeping.

While I was being hunted down like a runaway slave in the mountains, my mother, widowed then, took Juana, my sister who should have been born in Miami, off for a vacation in Acapulco. Later, when our victory was assured, she had herself photographed lighting candles in church for the safety of her two godless sons. When I passed through Holguín, close to our estate, on my triumphal march to Havana, she met me to complain that "a few *locos* trampled our new citrus fields." I told her that we had reports she was harboring what remained of Batista's local garrison. "Oh no," my mother assured me, "I just had them in for coffee."

Since my father's position had given her exemption from her social origins, she assumed my status would exempt her from the new social order, exempt her from the agrarian reform. We were all Castros, weren't we?

In Cuba today we have another motto: "Children are born to be happy." It makes the obvious unusual simply by stating it. Yes, yes, of course. Children should be happy . . . then why hasn't this affirmation been included in the great bourgeois documents with all their "rights of man"? The only inalienable right under capitalism is "the pursuit of happiness," which means a guaranteed starting block in a race run against one's neighbors, where the rich are given a ten thousand kilometer lead. The prize that's offered is gratification through isolation, a rising above the mass. Our prize is the highest reward of the revolutionary experience. The happiness we offer our children—*criollos'* children, cigar rollers' children—is the sacrifice of individual will.

"Aha!" I can hear the traitors in Florida screaming. "Here is the red dictator at work! He's just the self-flagellating son of a decaying class, making everyone equal under his whip!"

Let them scream. I will continue to invoke a world of shared burdens. I extol sacrifice not only because it drove my petty hatreds from me but because it is the necessary step in the attainment of anything that matters. Name me an outcome of value that does not require hardships. And name a human experience that has meaning without being shared. Each time we bend, each time we do something we hate to do, we are closer to real freedom.

If only I'd been raised with such values! I might not have taken the world on by myself. But would I have been so well instructed in persistence? Would I have appreciated my victories? For instance: would I have wanted an education so badly if I did not have a father who saw no value in it at all? Achievement is measured by its frustrations. A goal is defined by the obstacles met along the way, especially if the goal is perfection! That is the terrible twist, the prime contradiction of idealism.

PAUSE: IF YOU ARE AT WAR WITH YOURSELF, EXTEND THAT WAR

How could I have known any of this in the beginning? I was a monster of ambition, with scorn for anyone else's errors. I was just too quick for the world. I felt I knew everything everyone was going to do before they did it, could guess every word before it was spoken. I was a racer, lunging for the finish line, a split-second ahead of the pack; there lay my anguish and all that I sought. And I was certain there were others who shared my frustration and my powers. If only I could find them! I had to know: Where did they live? What did they look like? I saw an army of bug-eyed, barrel-chested bullies, duplicate Fidels, distributed over the globe by divine calculation, eager to display their superiority, ready, at a coded command, to walk through walls.

Was this my first yearning for the Leninist vanguard? I suspect that it was only my first yearning to find out I could be just like everyone else. I carry this fervent wish with me now. It would be so pleasant to be snoring contentedly like the rest of the men. Why not? It's already past three o'clock! But Alejandro must talk on. From day one to this numberless night, I have sought proof of my existence through a dialogue, even if that dialogue is with a machine.

And what the rest of them don't know is that I talk to drown out that other talker inside me. I think of him as a miniature and the very opposite of me: well-manicured, dapper, lithe. He sometimes wears a derby hat. Yet he has hung onto me along every curve of my remarkable ride. He is the remnant of my aristocratic haughtiness. He is the evil whisperer. This loyal *compañero* of mine has one job and he does it well. He informs me, "Fidel, the masses are nothing but a stampeding herd. They are the weak ones, the ones who don't want to have a choice." He orders me, "Look at their fat fingers, their deformed feet, their stained overcoats, their excuses." He tells me, "Listen to them whistling their borrowed melodies. You and I know, Alejandro, that this is not a world for whistlers." He asks me, "Can you forget about injustice? Why should they be allowed to forget?" He whispers, "This love of the people condemns you to mediocrity. It slows you down, *amigo*. It is your dilution."

The only way to quiet this recluse is to let him have his way. As a boy I resisted and the creature fed on my resistance. I tussled with him all night. I sharpened my debating skills on this invisible opponent. I had not yet identified him as the self-love I could not bear to sully or share. From the singular to the mass, the one to the many: on this fulcrum we sway, pushed by our dread of what we are or are not. I couldn't have known that dread is the companion to any full effort, that the pettiness inside me was a preparation for generosity.

I did know to keep moving. Each time the voice sought to paralyze me, I threw myself more completely into action. I smashed a window. I incited my mates. I dove into the collectivity. I sold myself to the world, and never one to haggle, I sold myself cheap. When requested, I gave myself away. I took up every cause. A pension for gravediggers! An allowance for my sister! An indoor toilet for our dormitory! I wasn't fussy. The cure for my elitism was real life, a cure recommended for all parasites. Swallow it down. Maximum strength, repeated dosage. And if you have to ask what "real life" is, you do not need to seek it.

I sought it among the fishermen of the Bay of Nipe. How old was I when I first ran away to the sea? I had tired of climbing mountains. I was trying to grow my first mustache. I knew how to ride the box-cars of sugar. The closer I got to the bay the more deeply the River Mayarí cut into the plain. The squares of fallow soil got blacker. More and more of what grew was tobacco, flapping its emerald wings. The long-necked palms craned higher than ever, like antennae for moisture. The landscape was a green towel, suddenly unbleached. Then I saw why. How quickly Cuba ended, and how decisively! So there was an uncluttered horizon! So there was hope!

I always treasured that first glimpse of ocean. I don't share any *guajiro* superstitions when it comes to our waters. When you live on an island, you had better not fear your only means of escape. I have always felt at home in the deep. When you live on an island, there is no better place to do your thinking. No matter what time I reached the first white lip of beach, even in the moonlight, I would take a long swim. I would dive as often as I could bear, though now I'm equipped with a tank on my back and a spear in my hand. Just today I was reminded, as I delighted to be reminded when I was fourteen, that there is no peace anywhere, not even beneath our clear waters. But I can choose to stay out of this fray. Though I carry a weapon for sport, I'm just as pleased to remain an onlooker in this underseas struggle. Breathing through my lip piece, I can issue no directives. I am reacquainted with pure oxygen. I am invigorated by renewed evidence of my dependence on the elements. I become merely another creature of the reef, merging with the azure diversity. I am welcomed by our nation's true neighbors. If the peasants could only see that cavalcade of fish! I tell you, man lives surrounded by hallucination.

The fishermen knew this, though they did not have the words to articulate their understanding. They showed it through calm acceptance of all hardships. They even accepted me! If I got to the docks early enough, they would gladly take me out with them. They let me cast out their nets. They answered my innumerable questions about their methods. Here was another source of astonishment for me: this was how people put food on their table! From watching my father, I thought it was done only through scheming. I enjoyed the fishermen's company even more when they passed 'round stone flasks of homemade *aguardiente*. When I was flush, giddy on a becalmed sea, I would babble on about the need for a truly representative government. I was big on the "true definition of democracy, as derived from the Greeks!"

The fishermen had no time for Greeks or true definitions. They were gauging the winds, scanning for gulls and traces of marlin. They were the most quiet of Cubans, the first I had met who did not have ready opinions on all topics. But their silence had nothing to do with awe. They were not merely humoring me. No, they appreciated my fine words just as they appreciated my formidable breaststroke. Both proved I was a rich man's son. When they asked me for my father's name, I would tell them, "I have only one true father. His name is Martí."

That should be a clue to my age! In the throes of puberty, I had discovered the attractions of that melancholy maiden called a free Cuba. I swooned over her with the help of Martí's love poems. And I had not come to know this man merely through his writings—though he wrote as I speak, in torrents—but through dreams, where we meet our true forebears.

And Martí was the reason I met Pérez.

At the mention of the great poet, they led me to this old fisherman. He lived on the beach in an oversized tin of anchovies, a blind man repairing nets. In the midst of that brilliant sand, here was a square of darkness. I could see the room was clean and hung with a variety of clocks, wooden and brass, and a cuckoo. The clocks were all stopped. I remember post cards and exotic cigarette packets tacked to the walls' burlap lining: the bounty of a sailor's sad voyages. At the back he sat in a rocking chair, in *espadrilles* and a blue tunic, hands working away, lips locked in a frown, hairless and quite sightless.

What did these ignoble surroundings and this blind man have to do with Martí? I was sure I'd been tricked.

"They told me I could find my father here," I snapped.

And I heard the old man declaim forcefully: "'Don't put me in the dark to die like a traitor; I am good, and like a good man I shall die facing the Sun!'"

I was shaken, but not speechless. "'If they say: from the jeweler, take the best jewel, I take a sincere friend and put love aside.'"

The reply was more Martí: "'Every Cuban who falls, falls upon our hearts. The land itself is what we need. Having it, where is hunger and thirst?'"

I would not be outdone. "'Palm trees are waiting brides, and we must establish justice as tall as the palms!'"

The fisherman tried to rise, but I stooped to embrace

him. Since the great poet had made the introductions, we had presented one another with unimpeachable credentials. But while I could recite Martí, this old man had actually known him, touched him, fought in his tattered regiment on the day he was killed. With my help, the fisherman found a faded call to arms that had been folded in his wardrobe for thirty years. Here was another wonder: the War of Independence had not just taken place in books! I almost drowned Pérez in questions.

"Did he carry a notebook? Was he good with a rifle? How did *El Apóstol* die?"

"He was killed by his own eloquence," Pérez answered. "His speech to the troops was so lengthy that the Spaniards sensed his position. But no one would have dared cut Martí short. He led the counter-attack, but fell trying to reload his weapon. It was probably jammed anyway, from improper cleaning. He took a shot in the vest pocket."

Pérez said the bullet broke the watch that had been given to Martí by Horace Greeley of the *New York Herald Tribune*.

"I carried the body away. It was light as a bird, as if the man's fire had been extinguished, his insides gone to ash .... He was slight, his complexion nearly bloodless. Martí always looked like he was about to faint. His wispy hair would never stay down on his forehead. But his eyes burned like kerosene lamps."

"He was not like the rest of us," Pérez told me. "Not like the lumbering Cuban, with perspiration always beading on his upper lip."

In the darkness, Pérez touched my lip. He felt that I, too, was sweaty there.

"Why is it we can't get used to the heat we know all our lives?" The *viejo* asked and answered himself. "We're a race of orphans. This island orphanage must become a real home."

"My book said that Martí died taking ten enemy soldiers with him . . . ." I was very disappointed.

"Martí put too much faith in his visions, but visions do not win battles." I was not disappointed by this old man.

All summer I returned like the tides to the hut of Pérez. I welcomed the days when I could hide from the sun and find illumination in this man's darkness. His appeal was further strengthened when I saw that he took my future leadership for granted. In his presence I did not have to fight feeling special. For the first time I could ask aloud, "Must I carry the fight by myself? In other people, in the world they have made for me, I find only disappointment and deceit."

"If other people oppress you, other people are what can set you free . . . ."

"But I'll tell you what perplexes me about history. It's not that people can be moved to action, will seek their betterment, are more than willing to take up rebel arms, but that so many through each epoch are content with so little, defend what they do not own, fight to remain enslaved, fill the armies of causes that are plainly bound to lose."

I even kept Pérez posted on my dialogue with the little man inside me. The old man quieted my self-doubts.

"Now you have the proof that you're not so different from those people you bemoan, the people you must lead . . . . You too are selfish and short-sighted. You are intolerant. In short, you are imperfect. Didn't you know it, son? The damage this society does it also does to you. All the more reason to act on your own behalf, not just in the name of others! If you are at war with yourself, all the more reason to extend that war!"

Until I met Che, Pérez was the only man to warn me about the spectre of perfection. This would be my major adversary. Nothing could be more destructive than expecting too much of myself, too little from my followers. Pérez had seen his own generation overtaxed by unreachable standards of conduct, burdened by fine words in foreign books. They were trying so hard to be Cuban George Washingtons, Cuban Robespierres, that they forgot what they were fighting for.

"The great bluff," that was what Pérez called it. It would take me many years of bluffing to know exactly what he meant. He meant speaking for the masses before knowing what to say. He meant reveling in invented triumphs and losing the taste for real ones. I understand this temptation. When a proud man has nothing, he takes possession of a negative form of property. Since he cannot proclaim, "This is my country, this is my land, this is my good woman," he substitutes, "You cannot take these things away from *me!*" He clenches his fist but rarely swings it. He learns to stand tall, largely to disguise the fact that he is creeping about on tip-toes. Why is he scared of his own footsteps? Who can hear him? Will the U.S. Marines come to spank him? How is it that he is guilty of trespassing upon his own land? These questions are avoided through ceremonial show. I often think of Pérez and his great bluff when I attend international conferences of "emerging nations" and observe those sons of the *junta*, who emerge like exhibitionists, waving their armies like genitals, quivering under their epaulets and medals. I, too, have a taste for epaulets and medals.

The old fisherman did not want me to join the ranks of those insecure generals. He made me repeat over and over Martí's ultimate warning that "all the world's glory fits inside a single kernel of corn." Pérez was my first teacher. That tin shack by the Bay of Nipe was my first real school. At last, I was being asked questions for which I did not have quick and clever answers.

"Is the glory of Cuba the same as the glory of Castro?"

"For the sake of independence, will you give up your name altogether? Will you throw away your books and their big words? Will you offer your smooth face, your firm Roman nose, for disfigurement? Will you yield up the strength in your arms, the speed in your prize-winning legs?"

Looking at Pérez, I could see that I might as well yield them up, since time would take them anyway.

"For victory," he asked, "would you let yourself be buggered?"

"And can you envision what we're all after as sharply as this blind man can?"

Once, just before summer's end, I got angry because I could not pass these tests. Pérez reminded me that I still had time to find my own answers. He sent me away with a last fillip from Martí: "All is beautiful and constant, all is music and reason, and the diamond, before it is light, is coal."

Pérez died at age one hundred, the year we took power. I ordered his body moved to the Santa Ifigenia cemetery where it rests beside the most honored martyrs.

By then, I had confirmed all his wisdom. I'd learned it all over again, through "direct observation." What a pointless exercise! Must each of us go through what everyone else goes through, as our spiteful neighbors wish? Why is it we can't simply accept the obvious truths of those who have gone before us? Why are human beings so suspicious of their own kind? I know I was. I accepted nothing. No one's complaints were ever as justified as my own; no one's pain was ever as great as my own. The blood of a dying man is only tomato sauce until we are the ones who are doing the dying. Socialism, real socialism, will come when we are all one heart, one skin, one wound.

PAUSE: A MOVEMENT BEGINS LIKE A LOVE AFFAIR

Until the Revolution, I wanted all the things I did not have and had all the things I did not want. But I never admitted it. I too took my place in the great bluff. Arriving at Havana University, I fancied myself a champion of the poor but I acted largely on my own behalf. And when I say act, I mean that which is done on the stage, under rose-colored lights, in a series of conventional postures. I'll never forget the curious flattery contained in my senior yearbook in-scription at Colegio Belén: "Fidel has good timber and the actor in him will not be lacking." If today I can extem-porize for eleven hours without an attack of nerves, it is only because I've had so much experience reading from a script that was not my own.

My entrance in Havana was dramatic—at the wheel of a cherry red DeSoto. It was my father's graduation pre-sent and embarrassed me mightily. I didn't want to accept it, didn't want to be seen around such ostentation. But what a V-8! Truly, I appreciate such sturdiness put to the service of man, even if General Motors is the source. A revolution may be continually in danger of losing its form, but a good piece of machinery is resolute, unmalleable, and wins its battle for mankind every time the ignition's switched on. This beauty negotiated all potholes on what passed for the National Highway. It was a convertible, too. I felt obligated to share so princely a phaeton. I gave rides to drifters and orphans. Peasants and their roosters filled the immense back seat. I had found a way to pay back my father: his bauble was now "Fidel's Bus." I was so gener-ous, I must have transported half the nation. But my mind was on impending academic glories. I slipped on a pair of dark glasses and practiced my public speaking by giving a guided tour.

"On our left, the city of Bayamo, twice burned to the ground so the Spanish would have nothing to conquer. Principal economic activities: cattle breeding and raising of sugar cane . . . . On our right, Santa Clara, capital of Las Villas Province. Principal economic activities: cattle breeding and raising of sugar cane . . . . In the distance, La Habana, bordello of the Caribbean. Principal economic activities: gambling, beggary and graft . . . ."

Though the atmosphere matched my own ebullience, I viewed our foreign-built capital as a pitiful construct, an enlarged shanty, temporary and extraneous when compared with Oriente's ever-patient, overworked earth. Havana was nothing but a bright, bespeckled tick, swollen with the peasants' blood. I wanted to wield my needle and burst it.

Oh, I'll admit the place had its charms. In the evenings the *bodegas* were full of political frenzy. You did not have to go far to find a good argument. Or a good supper, beef hash and fried plantains in the Chinese cafes. Walking the pastel maze of Compostela Street, you could look up to find beautiful young sisters, as yet uncorrupted, holding hands, giggling, smiling at you from their flower-wrapped balconies. But the intricate grillwork of Old Havana's balconies were the bars of my prison cell. The drooping red pods of the *flamboyant* trees were warning flares, nature's incendiaries.

When the tiles of the Prado turned cool with evening, the all-women orchestras played until everyone threw off their shoes and turned the promenade into a rhumba. But I did not join in. I was busy reforming the boys who sold lottery tickets—after I'd bought mine—busy organizing

59

the shoeshine legions, busy chastising the gypsies who trailed Yankee sailors, cooing for "Chiclets! Chiclets!" For the time being, I ignored the prepubescents who'd learned to sell their sisters, offering "private performances." There were too many of them, a legion of scrawny panderers. Along the sweep of the Malecón, down amidst the slippery breakwaters, couples made love openly. Those were the ones who couldn't afford to pay the cover charge of dark *boites*, where everything was allowed, everything displayed. Hieronymous Bosch could have set up his easel anywhere he chose. "Cubans, they say, are such an outgoing people . . . ." We were most outgoing when it came to indecency.

There were times I wanted only to hide out in my little walkup on San Lázaro. I had a mattress and a coffee maker and plenty of books claiming the corners like cobwebs. But real refuge came only at the top of the Escalinata, up those Corinthian steps, past the vigilant statue of "Alma Mater," under the marble columns that guarded the campus. It looked like a villa of some fallen emperor, not a university. I don't mean to suggest that there was no madness afoot here. It was just a sort of madness for which I was prepared.

I expected great things from the university but the university did not expect great things from me. I soon found out that this institution had nothing to do with learning, at least not in the usual sense. It was an adjunct to the government, a training ground for the elite, which meant that the most popular subjects were subterfuge and coercion. Student life, and the funds of the student associations, were controlled by the *bonches*, as many gangs as there were political opinions. The professors gave grades by group allegiance; report cards were held as payment for bloody favors; the registrar worked with a machine gun at his back.

The curriculum, for those who paid attention, had no more to do with Cuba than the Romanesque architecture. The textbooks all came from the United States. There was not a word in them that could explain the condition of Cuba or myself. Are you surprised then that I eventually went looking in the stacks under "M" for Marx? My teachers were all pedants. They wanted to drill us in *laissez-faire* economics and Unamuno's "tragic sense of life." Perfect preparation for a cabinet post! Splendid training for those who would oversee a country in ruins!

I wanted concrete knowledge. I aspired to be a man of applied science, though the applications were as yet unclear to me. But none of those who stood before me in the classroom knew more than any one of my tutors on the Bay of Nipe. At least a fisherman knows what type of bait to use, what hooks which creature.

I was outraged, but I was hardly conscious. I could not see a problem with the system. It was just that bad people were running the show. They had to be replaced by good people, like me. In the most venal city on the planet, living under the most blatant dictatorship, I kept blathering about the model Athenian city-state, forgetting about the large body of slaves that made such an experiment possible. With illegalities all around me, I vowed to become a lawyer. I honestly believed the law would moderate everyone, even me.

Fortunately, I could not adhere to any policies that stood in the way of my will. My character, spurious though it may have been, was perfectly suited to life in the capital. I was just like the ruling regime: I borrowed my urgency from the poor and my callousness from the rich. I knew none of the positive values of either. Though I exposed myself to all sorts of dangers to gain membership in the masses, my embrace of violence was just part of a youthful buoyancy. I was going to get everything. I would have my social reform and my career, my principles and my government post, my adoring followers and an adoring wife.

I was just like a hundred other brash, rising spokesmen of the wealthy. What saved me was that the other hundred would not accept me. I did not know the social graces. The high society in which I'd been raised had consisted of some Oriente policemen who came around to collect their bribes; many rowdy siblings; a few tadpoles. If Havana's workers found me suspect, the entrenched ruling class knew me to be a crude impostor. I can hear them taunting me in the univeristy halls, "Hey, *bola de churre!* Hey, Oriente bruiser! Come and show us those muscles! We got a job for you!"

It was some variation on this theme that caused me to pounce on the president of the student body. The black eye I gave him did more for my reputation than my term paper on Hegelianism. By the next semester, at the age of twenty, I was the president of the student body. So I stuck to my political illiteracy; my program was nothing more than a test of personal valor. As usual I was ready to take on all challengers. I stood or fell on my own. I was "El Jefe" before I had followers to bestow such a title. Fidel the strongarm, Fidel the *pistolero*, Fidel the gangster in search of ideological turf. How did I manage to act so confidently when I knew so little about my true situation? Or was that the reason I could? I am constantly astounded by this capacity for delusion, in myself and others.

Like the student radicals of today, like the self-styled "red guards," wherever they may be, I had difficulty telling gesture from substance. It got harder to tell when the gesture was murder. It does not matter if I actually did the deed. Why are the historians so curious? They know perfectly well that I aimed my sights on many a sentry during our war; this period was war undeclared. And don't you think someone would have told on me by now, in this cramped country where I can be reminded, twenty years beyond the fact, of an overdue library book? No one is going to find my prints on a snub-nosed revolver, though my fenzied oratory may have sent my cohorts off on head-hunting missions. Listen, *chico*, my aim was to stand out from everybody else. If they were shooting it out with each other, why did I have to?

When my enemies tried to pin the shooting of Manolo Castro on me, friends told me to hide, they told me to run. I got as far as the beach of Santa María Del Mar where, after a brisk swim, I decided to turn myself over to the police and face the slander head-on. The threats of my enemies only made me appear more powerful. The plots above which I could rise only made me appear more no-ble. I cornered the market on morality. I learned to be so scrupulously treacherous, so consistently inconsistent, that the struggle itself became my sole confidant.

Yet I make no apologies for my youthful impulse to revolt. I will never renounce it and no one else should. Don't let those in power make you feel foolish or contrite, not until every condition that prompted your first protests has been wiped from the globe!

A movement begins like a love affair. You do a lot of crazy things, take a lot of meaningless risks. You throw ice cubes at visiting Yankee lecturers, escort a recruiter for the State Police off campus by shoving a toy pistol in his back! Later, life gets more serious. But I received my train-ing disrupting ballgames, distributing handbills during blue movies at the Shanghai Theatre, speaking from soap-boxes outside casinos. To get noticed, I learned to raise my hand above my head like a flamenco dancer. I kept a white suit clean so I would look properly pure. But I too was dependent upon the existing evils. I didn't really imagine they would ever disappear!

I needed something to scream about, to spur me on. I required material for my student radio program. *"Escuchamos* Fidel Castro Ruz with music, sports and commentary on events of the day...."* What a holler I put up when Josephine Baker and her formidable negritude were refused a room in the Hotel Nacional! And what about the increase in bus fares? These were earth-shattering issues. My proudest moment came, as always, in the form of a prank. Borrowing my fare, I went to Manzanillo in the middle of the night and stole La Demajagua, the Cuban imitation of the "liberty bell." I hauled it back to Havana on the train—a feat for a weightlifter, not a propagandist—then displayed it all over town, staying one street ahead of the police. When I rang that bell, I let everyone know that liberty in Cuba was dead. And that Fidel Castro was very much alive. And so were his *cojónes!*

Which leads me, or led me, to Cayo Confites, a barren reef one kilometer long. This "candy key" was a piece of melting coral nougat, a slippery nub that did not deserve to bear such a gay name. I did not deserve to find myself clinging to it. Yet in 1947, about to turn twenty, that was "how I spent my summer vacation." I was one of twelve hundred bivouaced recruits in a self-proclaimed "Army of American Liberation." Pistols in every pocket, we planned to sail into Santo Domingo, where we'd unseat Trujillo— then it was on to Somoza in Nicaragua, on to Panama, on to *Nueva York!*

Our dictator Grau had promised to sponsor the expedition. What better protection could he afford himself than to aim his rabble at one of his colleagues? Or had he concluded it was more profitable to leave us all stranded like Robinson Crusoes? Two days on Cayo Confites became two wretched months. Here was the Left at its worst: adventurist, isolated, ill-prepared, waiting to be rescued by forces that shared none of our long-range interests. On Cayo Confites, I learned that the dead are lucky in that they do not have to wait.

I learned how to tell the difference between a vanguard and an *avant-garde*. Our plans were so stunningly foolish that only foolishness could have justified them. That bourgeois existentialist, Beckett, might have written our dialogue: "Are they coming today?" "What?" "The ships." "The ships?" "They're supposed to be coming today." "What for?" "Or did they pass yesterday?" "Who can remember?"

I also learned that one should never enlist in an army that has only one tent. The *comandante* will invariably take it for himself, especially if he's Rolando Masferrer. An expert on treachery, he would later outdo himself by staging that most unsuccessful of invasions, at the Bay of Pigs. While he got a roof and instructions on the radio, his troops got thunderstorms and rumors. An armada of mainland flies had followed us out to sea. The rations we'd brought along were rancid. When they ran out, we danced like Tropicana girls! Then we noticed our new home did not support the growth of any vegetation, edible or inedible. No coconuts, no *fruta bomba*, no shade. Our staging ground became a torture chamber. Our army was defeated before its first combat.

Though we fancied ourselves a powerful river, risen over its banks to cleanse the Americas, we were just a dirty pool gathering at the many drainpipes of the student movement. The solidarity we shared was a longing for the dubious comforts of our bohemian quarters, our noisy cafes, our overdue assignments. We did not miss the rattle of dice, the black market, the sectarian squabble. We had brought our favorite vices along.

Those nights on the reef, atop my first sleeping roll, in my undershorts, I had no more need of sleep than I do at this moment. But there was more to see on Cayo Confites, no separate cabins. I was able to observe moonlit acts of pederasty and perversion. The reef was like the Havana nightclubs I would not frequent. I was not entertained, I was horrified—not so much by the lack of morality as by the lack of discipline. It was such a waste of strength and zeal! And I nearly gave in myself, though not in the sexual sense. What I mean is that I paced and cursed like the rest. When the flies pecked at me, I allowed them to peck away at my ideals. That is the gravest error for a guerrilla. The validity of what he believes has no relation to the difficulties he encounters in implementing those beliefs. Yet there were moments on Cayo Confites when I wished I could be anywhere else, anyone else!

However, I soon passed the first threshold and began to savor my deprivation. I felt relieved when I could no longer placate my demanding persona. I stopped responding to my craving for a fragrant cigar, a fragrant woman, or a less than fragrant crowd cheering me on. Those were all cruel manipulations. And the cruelest manipulation of all, the monthly stipend my father still sent, could not reach me now that I was marooned. I had finally escaped my own "welfare state." The red DeSoto was suddenly obsolete! This seems laughable now, but I had to show myself and my family that I could survive on my own.

On Cayo Confites, I had to survive without food or shelter. My father, insensitive as he was, could never have punished me as I was now punishing myself. Was I doing penance for being an unworthy son? Or for wearing the mantle of my father's doggedness? I certainly did not feel like a criminal. I did not feel psychologically sick but that I was suddenly well. If I was driven by a compulsion, it was not mine alone.

And what was that compulsion? *To be free.* So many have raised the cry and meant so many things: freedom from persecution, freedom from taxation, freedom from neckties. Certainly, in Cuba we sought all the usual categories of independence. We wanted to run our country for the sake of ourselves and not foreign interests. But that is only extended selfishness and freedom is what we get after we have stopped being selfish. Like everything we want the most, freedom is what we understand the least. It is hiding somewhere on the other side of where we say it is. The truth, after all, is unalterably divided into halves: the half that is and the half that is yet to be, the half that remains and the half that must crumble, the half that meets our eyes and the half that will never be visible. This is confirmed through eastern duality or western dialectics or the primitive rending of the sky into heaven and hell. But how can we live in service of such an awareness? How can we act on the basis of what is *not* before us rather than what is? How can we appreciate the view around the corner as well as the view that is before us? On Cayo Confites, where the view was blank, limpid sea, I first made the acquaintance of freedom. For me, freedom has never meant being free from the constraints of others. It means being free from the constraints of myself.

The longer our army was trapped, the more I felt as I had the night Raúl and I scampered into the Mayarí Pine Grove. We were all wild beasts, and like beasts we were obliged to survive for the sake of something we could not name. My spirits rose day by day. I tried to lift my *compañeros* up with me. "No more dominoes! It's time for morning inspection!" I made everyone clean their rifles and themselves. I led drills and calisthenics. "Hup, two, three. *Uno, dos ... Venceremos!*" I wish I could still do those sit-ups!

With Pedro Miret, a friend from an introductory class in sociology, I formed an honor guard of the reef. Together, we marched ceaselessly from end to end. Years later, he would steal a Yankee transport plane and land a crucial shipment of arms on a *Batistano* airstrip. He may have been inspired by the way we had talked to bolster our morale.

"What matters, Pedrito, is to do something, do anything."

"But are we doing anything?"

"We have entered the world of events, which is inevitably the world of force."

"Then force must be nothing more or less than attending to details. *Por ejemplo*, the removal of these sea urchin spines from between my toes."

"We have taken the first step. Our fists are out of our pockets. If we thrust them into a wall, that's only a reminder that we will soon find softer targets."

"For our generation, mistakes are advantages in disguise."

"Sometimes it is less important to know what we should do than it is to find out what we cannot do."

"Like shaving, Fidel?"

Truly, that was how we became "bearded ones." Our new image would be rooted in concrete reality. We had forgotten to pack our Gillette razors for the trip—the next time, we would do so on purpose—and so our hormones asserted themselves. *La barba:* not an insignificant matter, but something tangible, a prod whose itch added to your itch, a prop that made you unfamiliar to yourself. At first, I was pleased simply to hide my double-chin. The ideological content was left unexplored. It was in the Sierra Maestra that we identified the beard's many dividends and began to cash them in. For a start, we found that it was problematic for a spy to infiltrate us unless he'd been cultivating his whiskers for some time. Then again, the beard was a better advertisement than anything they could have cooked up on Madison Avenue. Right there, under our noses, we found free entry into the realm of myth.

True, the beard was a well-worn trademark for masculinity, strength, and authoritarianism unabashed. That suited our purposes at the start. We might have been frightened kids but we looked like patient, responsible elders. How could we disappoint the people or ourselves? At the same time, the beards remained a symbol of opposition to the corporate eunuchry being imposed on Cuba. We would not be clean-cut and "up to date." Our hairiness made us prehistoric: we would go forward by going back. We would club the past into dust and begin at the beginning again.

Today, my dusty appendage reminds me that we have more clubbing to do. One tug on my chin and I remember that we did not get where we are in the space of a few shaves! The Cuban masses must remember this, too. That's why I'll never be shorn—and I hear the beard grows after death, too. As long as the beard is in view, so are the means by which we seized power: our embrace of hardship and our use of nature as a shield. But then nature gets its revenge. The beard just happens to be the first place where grey hairs show themselves! That bothers me, I admit. I don't want to look older than I am, though I do get to look much wiser.

Showing my age was the least of my worries on Cayo

Confites, in the days of my first stubble. The dreadful affair came to an end when three Cuban navy frigates steamed along and scooped us up. I will never forget the name of my slow boat: *"La Fantasma."* Most of our dehydrated brigade still believed we were headed for Santo Domingo, but few were truly surprised when the ships turned to the starboard, back toward Havana. Word soon followed, already redundant, that the government had withdrawn its support for the expedition. But a second rumor swept through the crowded deck: Emilio Tró, a leader of the faction with which I was temporarily aligned, had been gunned down in the streets. Only Masferrer's gang could have done it, striking just at the moment when their rivals' muscle, including me, was occupied elsewhere. Not only would I face the police on my return but I might also face an attempt on my life. This was one homecoming I was eager to postpone.

As the historical record shows, I am the only man who came off that reef and was not arrested. Not bad, eh? When night fell, I crept out of the holding tank in the hull, found a raft to throw overboard, then threw myself over too. This was the first of my fabled escapes and certainly the simplest. I'm sorry to admit that I did not have to evade a hail of machine-gun fire. The navy was more than glad to lose track of one lunatic more or less. I just paddled off, using my big hands. I carried no rifle on my back and I did not swim twenty miles to shore, as so much apocrypha suggests. I do remember ditching the raft for the last few hundred yards. Frankly, I needed the exercise. I wanted to regain my form in the breaststroke. Possibly I was hoping someone would see me—evidently they did—grounding myself foolishly but heroically, a whale in fatigues. As for the very real sharks in those waters, they did not frighten me as much as the human sharks in Havana.

What had Pérez told me? "Imitations are always more extreme than their models."

In such a manner, I returned to my homeland to take up the study and practice of law.

PAUSE: A LITTLE CHASTITY GOES A LONG WAY

On my way back from "the front," technically a fugitive, I took the opportunity to stop at the Castro *finca* and fatten myself up on our maids' cuisine. I had quite a juggling act going! Textbooks and ammo belts and silk shirts, all in the air at once. I was a living case, a victim, of Engels' "combined and uneven development." And my lag in consciousness was rooted in economic relations. You see, I lived off my parents until I was twenty-six, until prison put an end to the charade. One side of my mouth ate from the surplus value of the *campesinos*, the other side spoke of their suffering. In my gleaming DeSoto, I drove to anti-American rallies. With my allowance, I bought the revolver that would be pointed against my benefactors. There was plenty left over for bullets. Accepting my personal student loan, I sharpened the legal acumen that would also be turned against them. I thought I was very clever, but all the while I was keeping myself colonized.

My financial dependence kept alive all sorts of ridiculous notions about repayment. I would be my parents' slow-accruing trust fund. I would return to lay a sack of dirty dollars on my father's desk. Lay it on his head.

It is so fatiguing, this jousting with our birthright. So many become the creatures they abhor. So many lose the fight, and they do not lose it in the sunlight of battle, smitten for all to see, but in darkness where their dreams are corrupted.

Like the child who has been beaten, I sought to beat. Pure rebellion, rooted in a childish faith in one's own perfectability, ends up paying homage to all it hates. I would earn money more efficiently than my father; I would be a more capable spokesman for his greedy nationalism; I would find myself a prettier Señora. Yes, above all, I would become what my insensitive father could not be: a good family man. What a detestable phrase! That is what they say at the funeral of someone who has failed to do a single remarkable thing in his life, who has merely tended his own garden. He was "a good family man." Yet that was what I was striving to be for so long, what kept me from reaching the collectivist course.

"And where did this Señora come from?" The world's flesh peddlers, sometimes disguised as political commentators, have been dying to spring the question. They have probably been listening to this tape at "fast forward," skipping to this point.

Do I have to satisfy them, Celia? "Satisfy me," she would say, "and you will be satisfying yourself."

Yes then, Celia, for you. You are the only one who has the right to know.

But I would rather not dwell on the grim mechanics of courtship. It is not cowardice but a sense of dignity, the dignity of our cause, that make me self-censoring. I am like one of those old Hollywood tycoons, invoking the least ambiguous of moral codes: "One foot on the floor at all times, please—even during the procreative embrace!" I will not let the camera show my wife in a prone position. If it did, it would also show me down there on the mattress, grappling.

To get the plot rolling, I can tell you that Mirta Díaz Balart was introduced to me in a university cafeteria by her brother Rafael, a classmate and fellow member of the Ortodoxo Party. I could hardly believe she was a graduate student in the Department of Philosophy. She looked out of place among students—without notebook, with pearls—but that may have been her charm, or her fate. I would certainly take her into many crowds where she would be out of place. And her brother would regret his introduction as long as he remained in Cuba, which wasn't all that long.

The Díaz Balarts were fixtures in Havana society, though their ancestral home was in Banes, not far from where I was raised. Rafael was a wealthy scion with a wealthy scion's affliction: he was never quite sure how he felt about anything, never able to stammer out what he believed. Hence he found me appealing. And what did Mirta find appealing? Probably she was not told about my clandestine activities or my maniacal pals. She knew only that I was a brilliant student with a promising career. Brilliant, promising, but in no way bland. "Have a seat, won't you? Sit beside the next president of the law students' association, the last honest man in town!" Her brother may have blushed and told me to kindly close my mouth, but from our first meeting Mirta could tell I had plans for the long run. And Mirta Díaz Balart was a long run kind of girl.

She was not like the others I had known, not that I had known too many. The guardians of my manhood had done a splendid job. By the time the Jesuits got through with me, I had learned to perceive contact with the opposite sex as the purest and most effective form of pacification. An afternoon field trip with a girls' school, a moment in an unobserved clearing to grab some curly-haired nun-in-training and peck her on the cheek ten times, twenty times if some other boy held the record, best of all to dance clumsily at a social, filching a little warmth, these were rewards which the priests offered in exchange for our docility. Such experiences have undoubtedly colored

73

my view of that most overrated of social adventures.

It was always an adventure with these good Catholic girls! To get permission to see one beauty I'd picked out, I had to show my school transcript to her keepers. When this did me no good, I scaled the walls of her convent. Once inside, I was hardly given a Romeo's greeting. My *vita sexualis* would have to begin in less controlled surroundings, back at Las Manacas. I was no more than twelve. It was the day I was given my very own baseball bat. A Louisville Slugger, Rabbit Maranville model. The thrill of holding it was more memorable than the thrill which followed. I tried out my new lumber at a game with the boys in Birán. I was prodigious with the bat, but on a double I overslid second base and landed in manure. A local girl showed me to a shed where she helped me clean my trousers and helped with a few other things too. I had no idea what I was doing. She must not have either. When I got home and described my conquest to Raúl, he assured me that I had missed my target, that I had been thrusting myself into a space between thighs which was more air than flesh. He had proved his point by showing the anatomy in a book he'd been hiding. Damn Raúl, my squirrel-faced brother, he was always ahead of me!

When I arrived at the university, I found that nearly everyone had scored more points than me in this curious competition. But I didn't care; I was out for larger game. I couldn't be bothered with what others called "having fun." For me, that was always the most grueling work. Drinking yourself dumb, driving up and down honking your horn, attending parties to have conversations neither boy nor girl really hears, making "bedroom eyes," making promises meant to be broken . . . here was yet another religion, a strictly-defined series of rituals meant to deliver salvation. Often I could not get past the first sacrament.

I found such futility in kissing and squeezing and rubbing. After a couple of banana daiquiris, there would be a chase, the girl sticking out her tongue until she was caught, then curling her fingers around my ears as we fell on some shabby divan, followed by gasped encouragements about my "oxen shoulders" and my "vaudevillian eyebrows." It's easy to recall the compliments of passion, harder to recall those who bestowed them. One or two women of the Left, bookish types in pleated skirts and cotton anklets, eager to show their disregard for prevailing strictures, managed to drag me to a *posada*, that curious Cuban home away from home, where our encounters were brought to fruition without fuss, without fury.

How could there be fury when there was no affection, nothing that would pass for the delicious if artificially-induced solidarity of love? To do it without love is to do it without forgetting the sherbert that is melting in the shuddering Frigidaire. To do it without love is to do it listening to the traffic in the street and trying to guess the models from the sound of their engines.

Those treasured intimacies, held out as the ultimate form of personal expression, were really my most anonymous moments. I felt I could have been anyone, and I could hardly see the difference between various partners. What was the point in searching out the sultriest set of eyes in all those eyes, testing lips among those parched, split, nervously offered lips? This was one aspect of that spectre of perfection that Pérez had warned me about. This was the microbe of romanticism, spread to cripple us all. I have never succumbed to this beast—well, only once. Though the Revolution itself is an undeniably romantic notion, it was inspired by an insistence on seeing the world as it was, on noticing what was broken so that it could be fixed. When I looked at other people, I saw mostly flaws: worthy of observation, of bemused wonder, but certainly not the adoration that some women asked from me.

Some of which may explain why, when forced to perform, I developed the habit of being in a hurry. Yes, Celia, the disorder —in both senses—was with me back then. I always sought the next phase, even in bed. All of me hurtled toward completion; my most intimate parts were also my most impatient. Often I was through before I started.

My partners would try to reassure me or pretend they were satisfied. But in this one area I was content to be a failure. I simply didn't want to take part in activities that were beyond my conscious will. I didn't want that messy "life force" flowing through me unchecked. This was an elitist aim, I'll admit, but I wanted control over when I lost control. I wanted to choose when I'd be hungry, when I'd get tired, when I'd climb on top of a woman. I didn't care to pursue these matters in the haphazard way others did.

To undress, it seemed to me at the time, was to encounter a peculiar sort of enemy. And while men in a gymnasium locker room struck me as equally apelike and ungainly, if not equally equipped, women were so distinctive, so varied. One smelled like hyacinths between her legs, another smelled like sour mash, another like bubble gum, another like garlic, another like gunpowder. Martí was right when he observed that "the food of women is the extraordinary." In public life, I have tried to second this poetic motion whenever it is appropriate, particularly before the Cuban Federation of Women. But I have always been more enamored of the ordinary. There I find my travail, there I find my solace.

The opposite sex, like anything opposite, provided me with too many surprises. I wanted to be the one to entrap, to leak information selectively, to sneak in and out of town unannounced: all tricks I enjoy to this day. Yet after just one plunge, the communist women would tell me the saints' names they were saving for my offspring. And that was only the first ambush! The wife of one of my professors, so modern and free, seduced me to wound her husband, then blamed me when she was wounded by a Mexican abortionist. The incident left a scar on me too.

But the worst result of all was the way I felt when I was finished, after I'd let the girl "make my insect crawl." Yes, an insect, that's what the *campesinos* call it in their unerring use of simile. I never felt so erratic, so undependable, as when I was riding the male urge. In those brief lapses when I was "on the hunt," I forgot leafleting assignments, missed meetings and misplaced my passions. I was a man who could not be counted on. Is there anything worse that one *compañero* can say about another? And that male urge, untamed, cannot be counted on as the basis for establishing anything human, except babies.

The impulse of the penis can be so easily squandered in liaisons of no consequence. In this one aspect it is not so different from the impulse of class consciousness. In emotional or national liberation, a little chastity goes a long way.

It is a lesson learned quickly when you live in a brothel. That way one avoids infection, moral or otherwise. I certainly didn't want to share any ailment with the U.S. Marines!

This was before the clinic called socialism opened its doors, before all sores were created equal. This was before the Revolution's most crucial reform, when we ended the selling of bodies so we could end the selling of minds. Just ten years after my student days, we would start sending Havana's brutalized farm girls home. Today they milk cows, boil cane for molasses or just rest. Some have required a lifetime of rest and we do not begrudge them. Some cannot forgive themselves, though we've taught them to envision the global rape of which they were such a small part. No one can be told that their pain is something small.

In the old days, the "freedom fighters," the boys who carried snub-nosed revolvers and gold crosses and sinister nicknames, all found relief in the back alleys where their sisters in red dresses and black stockings sat in cubicles. One push and these *jebas* fell back like rag dolls on the straw mats behind them. My guilty comrades were always trying to get me to join them on these excursions, to lure me into a tacit endorsement. One evening, I recall they even tried "room service," sending the girl to me. I must admit she was delectable, a big-boned *mulata*, almost as tall as I was, with freckles and lips like pink saucers. I didn't care much for her blond wig, that skull cap of subjugation. In any case, I was not going to touch her.

"Who sent you up here, *chica?* Are they paying you well? Listen, go back to your village. I'll bet there's a *guagua*"—like "bow wow," what we called the old Greyhounds—"leaving tonight. I'll give you the fare."

The prostitute laughed. She'd never had a customer like me.

"You must not let the Yankees use you anymore . . . ."

"But I like Yankees. They are easily fooled . . . ."

"And how can you say that? They buy everything we produce at a low price, they sell everything we need at a high price. They have given us the Platt Amendment and the Machado terror and now they are reaching up our most intimate orifices, trying to split our last membrane of pride! How will our women see fit to have children when they can be bought by a Hershey bar? How will you produce the next generation?"

The prostitute laughed even harder. "... I can't have a child ...."

"Go home to your family! Go home!"

"But I can't. I'm a boy ...."

So I was the one who was easily fooled. Actually I was enthralled, sincerely awed by the illusion. When my dear friends burst into my apartment, hoping to catch me in some doubly damning act, they found me standing, one foot planted on a stool, sharing my last *Romeo y Julieta* with that poor specimen of the street, who was falling asleep in my only chair, listening to my lecture about "the marvelous ingenuity that poverty can breed."

I was past admitting that ingenuity could also be a by-product of lust. After three years in Havana, I felt smugly justified in my celibacy. Where everyone around me was procured or procurer, I removed myself from the market.

But that was before I met Mirta. Nothing I had learned seemed to apply to her. Though she came with a dowry and a watchful *duenna*, she was no commodity nor could she have seen others as commodities. She was so bourgeois, so above it all, that she had never been damaged by the more sordid aspects of bourgeois commerce. She was "civilized." This was one *chica* for whom I had to take my shirts to the Chinese laundry and get the tobacco stains off my molars. I couldn't impress her with snap-beads from the Havana Woolworth's. I had to learn my way around El Encanto, prowling in the lingerie section, hoping no one would recognize me though I cut a swath through racks of *peignoirs* while a few of my "boys" stood guard. The more I worked to win the regard of my task-master, the more luster was added to Mirta. Finally I had a fight I was worthy of: a fight to be worthy of her. I made a unilateral decision that this girl would bring out the best in me. She was going to be the good woman my mother had promised.

Coming from a raucous plenary session of some organization that could only meet in a basement, rubbing the ink from a mimeograph machine off my hands, I would call on Mirta and find sweetness, tolerance, serenity: all the attributes of the world I was struggling to bring into being! Returning to my larger battles, I would grip tightly to my memories of those moments with her, as if they were an amulet protecting me from harm. Mirta was my living locket, a hand-painted miniature, posed in a dress of a hundred lace layers. As the layers peeled away, carnality was reversed: the lace was whiter and whiter, the woman more and more pure.

The first time I held Mirta that dress of hers made such a loud crinkling sound, like burning cellophane. I hadn't meant to touch her. I didn't want to put her in any sort of disarray. It happened first in a movie theatre, of course. The film starred Robert Mitchum, one of Mirta's idols. That was a clue: she wanted a tough guy! But did she know how tough? I had gotten rid of her old chaperone by wearing her down, talking at her in a sweets shop until she fell asleep. Mirta and I ran all the way, so that we were properly breathless by the time we settled in the cinema's back row. In the protective dimness, I kept working my dancing eyebrows and my confident tongue. What a bunch of nonsense I spewed! Where did it all come from, this vocabulary of nesting? Expressions like "If I ever hurt you, I would hurt myself," and "In your eyes, I see all the good works we can do for one another." I was more astonished by my declarations than was my date.

Mirta was a formidable audience, always rapt. She made most of her points without talking. There were moments, especially when she was around her family, that she would make her eyes bulge, as if they were lights flashing, a sign that said: "Warning: Hypocrite Crossing." She had always been a jewel packaged in a tissue of lies, which gave her a sixth sense about all kinds of fakery. She may have accepted all the advantages of her class, but she sensed how stifling they were. That's why she fled into abstraction, studying such superfluous thinkers as Spinoza, Kant and Kierkegaard. That's why she could get so somber in the midst of the most frivolous parties. She was a subversive little pixie, "working from within." At least, that's how I wanted to see her. She was so quiet, gazing from her drawing room window at a floral Miramar street, or hearing me out at the back of a cafe, that I took her silences as endorsement. I would convince myself she was thinking about the fate of Cuba or existential man; she was probably thinking about cosmetics. But that's what a "loved one" is, what it was in the old days: the perfect mate was a perfect blank.

Still, Mirta must have agreed with me about something, about my taste in women anyway! She had grown up devoted to catechisms and birthday parties and washing behind the ears. It was not difficult for me to offer her a better faith. She tried sincerely in those first days to be a worthy convert. I exploited, and exploited with premeditation, that vacuum of convictions that so many women want to be filled. Her family had prepared her to become some fool's demure political wife, sitting loyally at the side of a rising young bureaucrat. I don't know who prepared her to become the capricious lover who bestowed and withdrew secret honors. "You are the sun, *corazón*. Take me home before I am blinded . . . ." For every part of herself that she gave to me, Mirta held a greater part in reserve. Was this her debutante's caution? Or was she aware that I required resistance, that she grew in my eyes as a moun-

81

tain grows when it is being climbed?

For a week or two—that was all I could spare—Mirta, not Cuba, was my cause. I stopped eating and sleeping, and felt all the better for it. I was back on Cayo Confites, denying myself, but this time the purpose was clear. I was in charge of the operation. I knew where I was going.

The people have a saying, that "Fidel is always assaulting the Moncada barracks." And my people, as usual, are correct. I am happiest when charging the battlements. If there were no more Moncadas anywhere, no more stone fortresses to bombard, I would have to construct a few. It is all horrifyingly phallic. I have my little battering ram, my heroic guerrilla of the groin. Would I could have a hundred soldiers like him! He does not question my strategy, yet shares in all my victories. He is with me when I smoke my long cigars, and make long speeches, and scatter my seed across our fecund isle. You see, that's what I've done with the urge that plagued me. Aside from its being rather obvious, what is wrong with such a solution? I say judge the results. I say all power to those who do everything with the urgent vigor of copulation! The future belongs to the sublimators!

But my future was in the hands of the Díaz Balarts. Their objections to me were strenuous and finally, openly insulting: "irresponsible . . . unsavory . . . freak of nature." Mirta would whisper these appelations at amorous moments. Her parents' disapproval was the endorsement both of us needed. It was so comforting and familiar, just like home. And the more I felt I was at home, the more I felt like being naughty. I didn't threaten to burn the house down, but I didn't have to. Invited for the most formal dinners I have attended outside the Kremlin, I would eat roast duck with my hands, drink Spanish bean soup from the bowl, then call for more while I berated the maids for

82

being so servile! At the same time, I would collect news-paper clippings for my future in-laws—"Young Castro Receives Oratory Prize," "Law Curriculum Needs Modernization, Says Castro," "Ortodoxos Nominate Castro to Head Youth Congress"—and send them along in the mails, signed by "an anonymous friend of the family." I didn't send them notices of my many false arrests. I knew that Mirta's parents would come to see that I was headed for notoriety. If only they could have guessed what kind!

They couldn't say no to me—no one ever had. Even if I was a bit clumsy, a bit reckless, a bit of a peasant, I had money and I had Mirta, my co-conspirator. And in a curious way, the Yankees were on my side this one time. In 1948, rich Cubans were falling over one another trying to be *Americano*, shrugging aside old colonial distinctions, hoping to encourage a "mobile society." I was certainly mobile, going forward with my usual disregard for all but the most delicious outcomes. I was grandiose, full of myself. Before seeing Mirta, I would stand in front of my bathroom mirror, combing vaseline into my mustache, screaming "Yes!"

In presenting my case to my future bride—and I saw her as just that from the first moment—I did not disguise my hopes and goals. I did not examine them too closely, either. I was going to win land reform in a case before the Supreme Court, then I was going to succeed Eduardo Chibás, leader of the Ortodoxos, as President, though he was not President yet, and then . . . I was in a hurry that made my customary hurrying look like slow motion. I was desperate, really, and my desperation was that of a pre-revolutionary trying to unearth some virtue in the world "as it is" that would keep him from leaping toward the world that might be. But I mistook this desperation for true love—which is not so unusual, since love is often an emergency attempt to relinquish free will.

In Mirta, I thought I'd found my second wind, but really I was never so tired, so worn down by my contradictory ambitions and beliefs. And I was not alone. That is what is wrong with biography, and autobiography: this premise that we move on separate tracks, that we chug along on our own steam. In 1948, many Cubans shared my fitfulness and my fatigue. We weren't model trains, we were more like wind-up dolls gone berserk. The best example of this came a few years later when Eddy Chibás was close to ousting Grau San Martín. One moment he was about to become President. The next moment he had shot himself because he could not wait. Was that normal? Didn't anyone notice how frantic we all were? Couldn't anyone calculate what it would take to make our collective spring uncoil?

Quickly, too quickly, I took Mirta for a stroll down the hypnotic curve of the Malecón, all the way to the puny ramparts of Morro Castle. Before those first conquerors' walls, we watched the sort of sunset that conquerors put on post cards. Quickly, I asked Mirta for the right to guide her destiny. I'd forgotten who guided all our destinies, that the post card sunset could not be mailed without a Yankee stamp. Quickly, too quickly, we were engaged.

Angel and Lina Castro were delighted by my sudden embrace of respectability. They insisted the wedding be held at Las Manacas so the city and country *nouveau riche* could be joined. Mirta and I knew it would be a fiasco, but how could we refuse? The Díaz Balarts, though insisting we record our marriage with their priest in Banes, found the whole idea "quaint." Their accommodations, off the pantry, were a little too quaint. My father was also at his quaint best. The smell of manure on his boots, the smell of pomade, smelly questions... "And how did you make your fortune, sir? What kind of pickpocket was your old man, eh? I'll bet you can't find cheap help like this in the city . . . ."

Mirta's parents were gone an hour after the ceremony. Fortunately, it took place in the main hall of our house and not in a chapel, since my father had kept his distance from the Birán congregation to avoid making donations. Unfortunately, the house was filled with every shred of human garbage in the province. Police chiefs in full holster, fat mayors in red sashes, field bosses, even the Yankee foreman of the *Central Miranda*, a bald buzzard in a seersucker suit who was known to have a thirteen-year-old Cuban mistress. He remembered my mother's bitterness over the share of our plantation's delivery that this man took for himself. But now she was proud to have him at her son's wedding. If it had been up to me, I would have invited my barefoot classmates, my old baseball nines, those who survived to adulthood. I would have sent out a notice to Pérez the fisherman, if he'd had an address. But I didn't concern myself much over guest lists and etiquette.

All I knew was that Raúl would be my best man. When the *finca* got too crowded with people we could not stomach, he and I took a walk down to the pond where we once abused the rights of frogs.

"You're getting old before your time, Alejandro."

"What do you mean?" I was twenty-one, he was sixteen. "I'm still faster than you are to the top of the hill."

"Not with a wife. A wife is too great a handicap . . . ."

I thought Raúl was jealous, but he was posting a warning.

"Let's go then!"

We raced up the nearest incline we could find. I beat Raúl one more time. I also returned to the wedding feast with dirt on the knees of my double-breasted suit.

Mirta just laughed when she saw me. She laughed at the dozen dogs on the porch, yelping in the Oriente heat, the goats whose farts could be heard through the floorboards; the servants swiping canapes, shoving them into their aprons when no one was looking; the village elders, hidden under straw hats, tapping their canes for the show to begin. My bride found everything comic, a fitting prelude to the tragic. And I found her stunning. How did someone learn to wrap their hair so tightly? I could never do it, not with all my strength. I could never be so meticulously bundled, so fittingly packaged, so respectful of my true self. Would she show me how it was done? Could I find all the answers I needed in this one demure oracle? Was the only requirement that I repeat an oath? "I take this woman" . . . I nab her, in broad daylight, in a stream of October sunlight . . . "this Mirta" . . . cruel anagram of Marti . . . "to be my lawful" . . . and awful . . . "to have and to hold" . . . my holy amulet . . . "to honor and cherish" . . . and hoard . . . "in sickness and health" . . . with sickness and wealth . . . " 'til death do us part" . . . *Patria o Muerte!* . . . and Mirta beaming up at me . . . "forever and ever". . . .

PAUSE: THE ESSENTIAL COMPONENT OF ALL HOPELESSNESS IS HOPE

Forever is not a Marxist word.

If only I could converse with that phantom groom pledging his phantom troth! I would have a question or two, a whole interrogation, for that sure-footed marvel, that impudent pup. I'd like to know just who that was under the waxed mustache, the clenched jaw, the flushed cheeks, the all-too-practiced, all-too-world weary gaze, beneath that helmet of hair molded by Brylcreem so that the path of comb's teeth was set in one rigid, ever-cresting wave. Everything I had been or was to become could be gleaned from my wedding day. Here it all begins, and ends. "The rest is history...": the kind they teach in school. History hurtles through us like a mountain stream, carrying fallen branches and dead ideas away.

And history has its unrecognized motives that must come to light. For just as a single man trembles and vacillates before the object of his love, or purposely acts to frustrate his own goals and capabilities, or turns traitor on the causes in which he secretly believes, so it is true with a people. With all peoples.

Among the Antillean breeds, we Cubans were once known as the Don Juans, the happy-go-luckys. Not really so happy, not really so lucky. We knew only blind rage and an eyes-open despair. We made a great show of our strong wills, then let the crucial decisions be made for us. Despite great bravery, which was often veiled suicide, the Cuban masses were particularly skilled at a perpetual postponement of their collective fulfillment. Even now, there are many who are frightened off by self-rule, who flee from the responsibilities of nationhood in their "freedom flotillas."

Yet today, after so short a time, Cuba stands as a symbol of the most extreme fulfillments. Our problems now stem from too many desires unleashed. The masses have become so attuned to their wants that if they asked me for the moon, I would try to deliver it.

Wasn't that what I told Señor Jean-Paul Sartre? It happened on a blustery afternoon when I took him for a ride in my launch. I was trying to run him ragged the way I do all my guests; I was hoping to keep him off his guard. But our outboard stalled in the midst of an impending storm. Since neither of us could show our apprehension, we behaved like important personages, discussing momentous topics. Two great men at the mercy of an insignificant squall! While we waited for a rescue ship I lit another cigar, Sartre tamped down his pipe. He let his single straying eye survey the turbulent green sea, as if those waters were the modern age and its atrocities about to capsize us. He had bothered me about the unfortunate censure of the poet Padilla. But once I offered him my line about the people and the moon, he praised me for my humanism.

An interesting "ism," eh, *chico?* As if it were possible to carry a membership card in this species without sharing an awareness of our fragility! As if the urge to help others, to calm trepidations, to piece together some significance in the face of monumental emptiness, were a kind of pedigree, an honor gained through rigorous coursework at the Sorbonne! How simple it must be to codify a moral superiority which is never put to the test! Let the Europeans have their humanism, a term for academicians to toss about. The Americas, North and South, have long experience with the results of that humanism and those results have been thoroughly inhuman, thoroughly barbarous. That is why it was easier for me than for Sartre to conclude that true humanism could not be based on the freedom to trade or the freedom to explore or the freedom to challenge religious precepts or even the freedom to think and create. The humanism of our new man is based on the freedom to need.

"Ah, that's simple. Follow your urges!" No, this is the most difficult task of all: to admit what one must truly have and act in pursuit of it. Just look how long it took me! Flexing my muscles, playing with guns, striking poses like an art school model . . . What made me so good at eliciting praise from those I could not praise, at seeking the respect of those I did not respect at all? And how many times can a man imagine doing something before he actually does it? I wish there were records kept on such maneuvers: a contest, world-wide. I would like to know if I would come out among the most or the least.

I'd like to know why human beings are the only creatures who have such a tough time finding out what they need. It's too easy to point the finger at capitalism, to blame the profit system for promoting general hysteria and thwarting individual clarity. The problem is larger. The problem is: when we finally get what we want, it doesn't look anything like what we thought we wanted. Life's rewards creep up on us, they aren't stripes of rank bestowed for seniority. I may have come to Havana for an insurrection, but there would be no insurrection so long as I was there. I may have married for love, or for power, but so long as I was married I would have no love and no power.

Everything that happens can happen again in reverse. Look! Even this insignificant tape recording is reaching that point where it will be all used up unless it's turned right around backwards. Energy displaced in one corner of the universe is bound to be replaced somewhere else, no? The laws of nature can be applied to the workings of a machine or a cause or a man. There is something of the farthest star inside this listening box. Inside me too, there is a little motor—and also a bit of the stars.

When I chafed at the inequities on my father's *colonia*, I should have known that the land he had taken from the peasants would be given back to them through me. When my father deflected my attacks by sending me to the best schools, I should have realized I could bombard him from afar as I never could from close range. When I spoke from a soapbox to the slot machine addicts who were deaf to my message, I was merely being assured that I would one day be speaking before an army of gamblers, at attention while I set the odds. When I matriculated from the school of self-acceptance, I was already aware that I would receive my advanced degrees in self-denial. When Batista sent me to the Isle of Pines to serve a twenty-year term, I might have known I would keep coming back here, nearly thirty years later, to serve out my own term, to be confined by a freely-given bondage. Whenever I wallowed in a rebel's exalted hopelessness, I ought to have raised a banner, proclaiming: "The essential component of all hopelessness is hope."

Which is not to say that happy endings are in store for all who persevere. The length of our casualty list disproves that contention. Being right does not insure that we will come through unscathed; being right is what puts us in peril. So we must dare to be wrong! In this most dangerous occupation of living by one's ideals, optimism must be included in the survival kit. Where there are no guarantees, we must clutch at intangibles for our safety. Taking chances that madmen wouldn't take, we must be mad enough to believe in our success.

When the *Granma* left Tuxpán harbor, a fishing trawler for eight, carrying eighty-two expeditionaries and all their hooks and tackle, hadn't we chartered a delusion? Chugging away from our last safe haven, slipping off in the darkness like a gang of rum runners, were we not navigating in the straits of lunacy? No compass could have guided us. Past the lighthouse, away from all Mexican spies and informers, beyond the last ears of the coast, we stood as one to sing the Cuban anthem. Seconds later, having mislaid our supply of anti-nausea pills, the full choir was harmonizing with seasickness. Over the side, in ensemble, we improvised the anthem of the country where we were really headed: a realm with no snug harbors, no offshore limits, no comforting boundaries. Ferried to our finest moment, we lay face down, trying not to retch, staring at the hardened squid eyes on the deck. Highly-trained cadres worked like galley slaves to bail out the bilge. The boat moved so slowly that I wanted to get out and push. Our destroyer was destroying us! The first martyr fell overboard on the night watch. The clutch died, leaving our self-proclaimed vanguard to drift toward liberation. Finally grounded on the beachheads of fate, we were two days late for the uprising and more than twenty miles from our collaborators. We were forced to ditch all our supplies for the campaign ahead. We had to trample through miles of mangrove swamps, trying to raise boots coated with pounds of loam, battling the elements that were supposed to befriend us. We were unable to tell where the unkind Caribbean ended and Cuba's inhospitable shores began. Yet when the Air Force spotted us and began picking us off, I was still able to shout, "Listen to the way they are shooting at us! Those are frightened men!"

Was this not insanity?

On what were we sustained in those first calamitous days, when we ate tomcats and measured our daily ration of water with one lens of Che's field glasses?

When those few survivors stumbled into each other atop the Sierra Maestra, starving and lost, I wanted to scream, "Shit! Let's go hide!" Instead, I announced calmly, "The days of the dictatorship are numbered. We have won this war!"

Was this not asking for the moon? That moon was so distant, so out of the question—so "out of the question" that twelve men brought it down.

In all accounts of our struggle, *la lucha gloriosa*, there is one point stressed over and over by those who hurled themselves at Moncada's stone intransigence, stayed afloat on the *Granma's* leaky raft, forded *El Turquino's* rivers of death: none of us knew what we were capable of doing until we were forced to do it. Each of the callow dreamers who followed behind me learned that they could perform the miraculous so long as the miraculous was demanded. Every man is the answer to a question. Victory to those who say yes!

Yet how was I able to ask them for more than they had? And what made my diligent dozen so willing to give it? My advice will never be heeded as it was heeded when it was so ill-advised. My orders will never be followed as they were followed when they had no order. My judgment will never be trusted as it was trusted by those I was condemning. My words will never be believed as they were believed when all belief was suspended. Yet the voice that spoke those words must be the same voice that speaks to you now . . . .

SIDE
B

Quickly, to continue what was barely begun. Is there no way to escape interruptions, pauses, an end to my allotted time? I'm suddenly eager to follow instructions. I have reversed myself, gone over to the other side.

Am I doing good, helpmate? Is this what you wanted, half-bride?

At your funeral, good Celia, I was respectfully, impeccably silent. I let subordinates eulogize. Hovering at the back of the hall, my beard needing a trim from your clippers, my fatigues needing the touch of your iron, I must have looked like some vagrant who'd just wandered in for refreshments. I could barely hear the speeches: "Major Sánchez forged a record of unparalleled tenacity. Born into wealth, she nonetheless gave all she had to the masses—as a leader of the urban resistance, member of the Central Committee, and right arm of our President . . . ." Right arm! You were my right ventricle. They might have added to your titles: grand wizard of cancelled appointments, national mother hen, the Revolution's number one *ama de casa*. "She gave all she had..." What an awkward business it is when a revolutionary dies so far from direct combat! They should give us the bullet! In those vile rumors, that's what some people said I did to you. Nobody can accept that we might go piecemeal, the way you did, Celia, lungs collapsed from smoking, and overwork. They won't let us wear out like interchangeable parts—even though that's what we aspire to be. But don't worry, Major. I could not have done any better by your memory than those on the dais. I know you would have understood why I had to keep quiet.

"We are both talkers, Alejo, who know when it is best not to talk. We value our secrets because we find them so hard to keep."

If you were here, Celia, I would not be concerned about undue revelations. If you were here, I would not be doing this at all.

Do you want me to end my days ranting at this automatic ear? Shall I address an empty dining hall? How can I find salutations suitable to the occasion? "Honored ghosts!" (applause), "Distinguished shadows!" (great applause)... At least I don't have to sit still before a typewriter and confront the inhuman cleanness of paper. An empty sheet is more frightening than Batista's torture squad. Neither ever coaxed a word out of me. But this recorder is more attentive than you were, Celia, and just as willing to follow me about. I can prop up this podium atop the ice chest, against the trunk of a patio palm or out by the batting cage. I can pace and strut and go through all the motions of oratorical courtship. Better still, this audience hears my blistering articulation but can't see the stern facial uniform I must don in its service. Nor can it take note of the bulge at my official uniform's beltline, the effect of the slightest draft on my thinning hair.

The only drawback is that tonight's speech is thrown to a crowd I can't gauge, a horde I can't transfix, a people whose hubbub is saved for other heroes. Future monitors will be free to infer their own messages from my open-ended phrases. They will mutter significantly, "This is what Fidel really meant."

But I don't want to be read between the lines, or on the lines. Let Lenin and Mao have the bound volumes. I am too much a man in motion to be reified.

"That's just your fear of what you cannot articulate." Yes, yes. If you were here, Celia, you'd be tearing through my apprehensions like so much completed paperwork. "And your fear of the inexpressible suggests a fear of the intuitive, which might be a fear of the eternal, or the maternal . . . "

Very smart. I confess to all of the above. There are some fears that take longer to conquer than others; these are the fears we do not confront in the course of our work. But Celia, if you were so right about me in your intuitive, maternal way, why is it I never had any fear of you?

"I was not like other women because I was so like you."

It's true. The anatomical differences between us were quite incidental and we treated them as such. We shared ideas long before we shared bodies.

If you were here . . . .

If you were here, I might have asked you to offer me "the support of the skin." That was our little joke, and quite an infrequent one. It was difficult to concentrate on carnal tasks when so many others were bidding for our energies. It was equally difficult to consummate the traditional act when we knew the C.I.A. was a *voyeur*. In the capital, we had to move from apartment to apartment, bed to bed. No wonder I felt like a cocksman in a "live performance" at the old Shanghai. No wonder I didn't put on much of a show.

More than likely, you'd have stayed awake sitting here with me, helping me plot the next move in the Chinese puzzle of leadership, ruminating, matching me thought for thought, cigarette for cigar. You'd have propped up your feet on this very dining table, showing me the ballet slippers you preferred to boots. You'd have humored me, nodding away at my half-baked theories. All the while you'd have been sketching in the pad on your lap, drawing ideal cities, filling the glossy sheafs with endless architectural renderings of schools and child care centers, designing that sparkling, ordered kingdom that exists only in a spoiled girl's imaginings.

Like me, you were spoiled enough to demand a new world to live in. You were yet another turncoat in the class war. To show your seditious intentions, the secret police took a forged map marked with the spot of the *Granma* landing and wrapped it in one of your corsets! Your father, the plutocrats' doctor, fell for the ruse. He disowned you, but what did you care? By the time we joined forces in the mountains, you'd amassed fine credentials with the underground. I remember the advance reports: "Plodding, but a zealot . . . Alias: Norma. Code name: snapping turtle." You brought a dowry of courage to my second match.

Those earliest visits you made to the mountains, you were not merely "Norma," you were Florence Nightingale. You brought such mirth and also some much needed canned goods. It was not merely that you were a woman, though you were one of the first to share our guerrilla base. In the beginning, at Moncada, we made Haydée and the others stay at the rear of our attack and "play nurse."

In the mountains, ideology changed with need. We needed all the help we could get. And you gave it. Strangely
enough, you and the other urban operatives contributed a
special appreciation of our desperate trek. For you, the
mountains offered fresh air, clean fun, a vacation from
back-alley treachery. Between the two fronts there was a
magic symbiosis: we reminded you of the joys of the wilds,
you reminded us of the joys of civilization.

At the beginning, this was the excuse I gave myself
when I noticed I was trotting off into the woods to comb
my hair. It was absurd. Hunted down like a dog, I was
suddenly trying to look good, to look good for you, Celia.
Do you remember the first time you touched me, the time
you massaged my neck and shoulders while I soaked my
blisters in the *arroyo del infierno?* I was too tired to manage a response. My rifle was stiff for me.

After all, none of us had eaten in three days. Later, you
would take care of that. You became my personal grocer.
And I transmitted top secret messages, pleading with you
for more of that luscious split pea soup, the Swiss brand
in the foil packets, so bracing at the end of a forced march.
Batista's radio corps must have had fits when they inter-
cepted such a plea! The shopping list sometimes included
fountain pens and rifle grease. Or an urgent call for a den-
tist. If asked, you would have supplied a brain surgeon.

On your visits, you volunteered to transcribe my
manifestoes to the nation. They were much too long, as always,
but you copied out every redundancy. You also washed my
uniform and darned my socks without my having to ask.

Today, such behavior would be severely criticized by
your sisters; then, it won me over completely. In the hills,
our awareness of the damage done by sexual roles was as
yet incomplete. I am not ashamed of this. One battle at a
time, please, or none can be fought.

I suspect both of us were relieved that this battle kept us busy and away from each other. Even after victory, we tried to keep away. That was a hopeless cause, hopeless as the cause of the imperialists. So you became my "assistant." Still, I did not want to break any rules about fraternization, nor for the two of us to be seen together. We always agreed that our affection should not be a matter of public record.

This had nothing to do with prudery. It had nothing to do with your worthiness, Celia. You know that, don't you? I was merely setting an example—an admittedly tiresome business, but one that offers protection from all sorts of temptation. I was hoping, foolishly, to make the point that privacy was one right that would never be abrogated in our collective order. And let's face up to it: I was trying to keep something all to myself. Naturally, it backfired. The less importance I wanted attached to our "transitional arrangement," the more importance it attained through my uncharacteristic discretion.

In the end, my only enjoyment was keeping the whole world guessing.

I simply could not bring myself to endorse that archaic institution called marriage, that regimented selfishness called monogamy. This institution once gave me a hellish time; it continues to create all sorts of hells for our people. Yet how can I blame them for falling back upon such regimentation when I had occasional need of regimentation myself?

Is there a proper word in our hand-me-down language for what we two were together? Lovers? No, that finite love, the love of chivalrous ballads, was impossible for us. Comrades? A bit stodgy, too formal for the truth. Mamma and Pappa? I was touched by the way you doted on my son, but our children were everywhere and nowhere. Were we merely colleagues in the government, with a close working relationship? Were we secretary and boss, *amigo* and *amiga*, were we just Alejandro and Norma? What do you say, Celia? At least you will never suffer the indignity of having been known as my wife.

PAUSE: THE DUTY OF A LOVER IS TO MAKE LOVE

The first Señora Castro was not so fortunate. She came before the revolution, and a revolution teaches many lessons if we know how to take notes. In revolution, as in love, we learn that the pursuit of the desired object is more satisfying than its attainment. The means are an end, the machinations are all. In revolution, and love too, one party is bound to benefit more than another, true equality comes only in stages. It's quite useful to make such comparisons, to see both these struggles couched in the same terms. After all, love is the personal equivalent of revolution. For most people, it is their only opportunity to intervene forcefully in the lives of others, to change and be changed in the name of those others. But while it would be absurd to remind the people that "the duty of a lover is to make love," we are constantly having to remind them that "the duty of a revolutionary is to make the revolution." If only they could be aroused by the masses' hot breath! If only political seduction were a matter of wearing a particular negligee! If only long-ignored classes, abandoned nations, could flirt outrageously to get the attention they need, could cry out to be comforted and held!

Conversely: if only a man and his mate could beckon each other through diplomatic channels, exchange ambassadors, establish favored trade status, sign non-belligerency pacts!

But what precautions did I take, did Mirta take, when we forged our sentimental alliance? My memories of those first reckless days we spent together are both clouded and persistent. They are like a bad film that keeps returning to one atmospheric tableau, a glorified commonplace rigged with artificial lighting and artificial emotions. Yet it was all quite believable once.

This is our honeymoon. This is Miami. Florida! Where else do self-respecting Cuban couples go? It is a balmy Saturday night in Little Havana. We are dancing under the stars but the stars we see when we look up are bare pink bulbs strung around the back patio of a crowded *bodega*. We are walled off from Yankee prosperity by rows of manzanita and garbage cans and the back of a bottling plant. A jukebox with too much bass pounds out the stop-and-go of a Xavier Cugat mambo. I hear maracas, mocking horns, and lyrics pointedly banal, the better to separate their insincerity from the truth of the drums. "In Spain, they say *si, si*. In France, they say *oui, oui* . . . . "

But Mirta is actually listening to these words. She whispers them back at me as if romance can be learned by rote. Her hair falls weightless on my shoulder. For her sake I am pretending to dance, I pick one foot up with the beat and put it down right where it came from. I am in my dandy's see-through *guayabera*, with white lace flowers embroidered on the flaps, but it is creased from the poor job I made of packing our suitcase. My partner had chided me then. Now she clutches the shirt's slippery luxury and my sweaty back, trying to keep from sliding away, gripping me as if she might drop through some invisible trap door. I am hanging on too, squeezing all I can out of her.

There is no trap door beneath us, only a dance floor. It's not much of a floor, not nicely polished like the ones we provide in workers' clubs today, but a concrete slab broken in free-floating chunks. Since I don't know the proper steps, these slanted platforms offer me one more excuse to stand still. Anyway, this is a relatively slow number. Besides, the patio is teeming with couples. The oppressed are always said to teem, no? The oppressors, on the other hand, only mingle. And this oppressive overcrowding makes me feel as any bright young man must feel, that there are too many of us, so many duplicates that we are made to forget the value of originals. But these observations do not belong in my movie: just the determined men in their cheap, shiny suits that pulse, nearly phosphorescent, in the pinkness; the women in home-made gowns, fishnet stockings and glinting ankle bracelets beneath, eyes glinting too, the faces haughty and very much on display, camellias replacing curls in their straightened black manes. "Every little Dutch girl says *ja, ja*. Every little Russian says *da, da* . . . ."

In just three minutes of chorus and refrain, the single jerks, our conjugal tune is ejected. We continue without music, arm in arm. The spotlight moves to the principal players: I am wearing a fourteen karat wristwatch, slacks by Omar, Italian loafers with tassels. Mirta models a strapless summer dress adorned with a jade sea horse. Her brown locks fall from under a white planter's hat. Peering out beneath the brim, her Castillean eyes show no haughtiness, only doomed devotion. This crowd is too low class for her! But Miami has room for only one class of Cuban. Can't our beer garden compatriots tell that we are from the big island? That we are not two more orphans of the dollar? That we're not quite so skilled at pretending our lives are upbeat as *el ritmo?* That this is our honeymoon?

Luna de miel: it sticks to the tongue, sticky with secretions and platitudes. Both dry brittle in no time. Nothing is ever as romantic as it sounds: there's another golden rule, applicable to passion and politics alike. Especially applicable to Cubans arriving in Miami! I understand the expectations of today's "boat people" because I have hopped on that boat. The crossing is too rapid, too easily undertaken. Just ninety miles from despair to fulfillment, ninety miles from sacrifice to reward. So short a distance to bridge, and so many misunderstandings!

Less like a celebrating couple and more like refugees—that curious honorific reserved for scurrying rats—Mirta and I came off the ship loaded down with provisions. We walked the gangplank swinging plucked chickens that I'd slaughtered at Las Manacas. They were our board; for our room, we got no bridal suite in some geriatric palace. No, we spent our days of matrimonial exertion in an enlarged closet offered us by a certified public accountant who was one of Mirta's many *gusano* cousins. Even so, we soon found out, as future immigrants would, that we hadn't brought enough cash, that liberty came with a mighty pricetag. I did not enjoy wiring my father for emergency funds. One morning I was even forced to slink away from Mirta and pawn my gold watch.

Still, when we were in that grimy apartment we were not in Miami, we were in bed. With Mirta's head close to my flank, the ends of her hair slicing so gently across my protective shoulder, I was never so far from the events of the world. For once, I was able to take my time. I was rid of the "disorder." The magnetic charge between Mirta and me felt like a verifiable fact, the given result of a simple experiment, a reaction that had to occur, over and over, so long as we two were poured into the same vial.

Afterward, my bride would fall asleep with such ease that I imagined she must be the one creature on earth who had never been troubled by a bad conscience. As usual, I could not sleep at all. It was not more than a day or two before I started wandering into the kitchen to make a sandwich, or sending Mirta's snickering nieces out to buy me the Cuban-American dailies. I would read them, sitting up in bed, in a smudged undershirt, puffing cigars and stroking Mirta's brow.

Poor Mirta! She was just an innocent bystander in a time when innocence was impossible. My honeymoon with her soon became my honeymoon with the *Estados Unidos*. I took a mistress right under her nose! And this mistress, who could not be properly wed, could never be properly divorced. This "U.S.A." was to be my beloved adversary, my one true spouse.

I recall following the last phases of the 1948 presidential campaign. Yankee politics have always fascinated me: the candidates try to say less than one another and the winner is the one who says nothing. That is why the man Dewey was favored. He was absolutely without character. In Cuba, he could not have sold pencils on the street. But he was a Republican and Republicans voted for him. Why were they Republicans? They could not possibly tell you. Prosperity has bred this code which few can break. I confess that I can't.

Also, I could not resist the pennant races. I managed to catch quite a few games in a lively bar along Flagler Street. Television was the latest American miracle, and so was the fastball of Bob Feller. Still, I was disappointed to see him in the World Series instead of New York and DiMaggio, "El Yankee Clipper," then taking his final at-bats. My allegiance to the Bronx Bombers was further swayed by the Dodgers' Jackie Robinson. This player was the talk of the bar, as he had been the talk of Cuba. Now I saw why: it took *cojónes* to steal white home plate to the jeers of the racist mob. I envied Robinson his skills and his unique assignment. He would be the first big leaguer of his race: such a victory was indisputable, a matter of record. How could the men in that bar not help but salute him, when they were bench-warmers on the same farm team? And now that the Negroes did not have to pass for Cubans to get in the *mejores*, some *bona fide* Cubans could show what they could do. The men on either side of me wanted to know about our best prospects. I must have mentioned Minnie Minoso or Camilo Pascual. But I was thinking of myself. Between innings on television, and aided by several *maltas*, I dreamed that I called up that scout who had once been interested in me. It wasn't too late. I was only twenty-two. I did not have to go home and join a law firm. Naturally, I sprang from my stool when the men asked me to join them for an informal game in a city park across the street. The diamond was full of craters and dog turds, but I was impressed by the night lights. Inspired, I drove a few slow pitches against the stanchions. The men wanted me to join their league team, but I told them I would soon be back on the island.

"*Qué lástima!* What a waste of a cleanup hitter! Why do you want to go back there? Can't you see all the opportunities here?"

For once, I was being asked all the questions. They didn't seem worth answering. I had all the "opportunities" I could handle. I was a first-generation Cuban and I had no inclination to make my son a first-generation Yankee. One country, one battleground, was enough. I had yet to fully comprehend how the two were connected.

While Mirta dozed on, dreaming of a world that was all flowers and no fertilizer, I explored this connection. I had a few errands to run that were not strictly legal. If I had imported some Oriente chickens, I would be exporting Texas lead. I was very careful; I'd promised myself not to disturb Mirta's beauty sleep with an arrest. However, I got into trouble when I wandered beyond familiar territory. Downtown, trying to keep up my spirits in the face of those somber, unshakable office buildings, I went into the largest drugstore I had ever seen. It was very clean, with checkerboard floors, ceiling fans and a lunch counter. Even the candy, the sodas, smelled like linoleum. I started to buy Mirta some perfume, but I was soon drawn to the magazine rack. There were magazines on every subject. It seemed to me that each brand of opinion, each attempt to be different, had been quickly packaged, converted into a sales item. If I had led a guerrilla army in the Colorado Rockies instead of in the Sierra Maestra, no doubt my march to victory would have been preceded by guerrilla trading cards, guerrilla fashions, bearded guerrilla dolls. I would have been asked to endorse White Owls!

The magazines were one-third journalism, two-thirds advertisements for new model cars. I was enjoying a spin around the block in each one of them. Then a clerk grabbed me by the shoulder. He looked like a Marine out of uniform. He was trying to heave me outside.

"No browsing allowed . . . ." Or was it "no Cubans"?

I summoned the words of Martí: "I lived inside the monster and I know its entrails; and my sling is the sling of David."

Luckily, I did not reach for a sling in that drugstore, or I might have spent some crucial years wallowing in the Dade County Jail. For once, I would not let myself be provoked. For the first time, I withdrew to fight on a better day. What made me back off? Mirta, my career, "circumstances"—the materialist version of fate.

To make sure that I behaved myself, I started rousing my wife and taking her with me on my restless jaunts. Roving the longest and bleakest boulevards, past wrecking yards and country clubs, laundromats and canine cemeteries and shopping malls in the form of Elizabethan castles, I kept my arm wrapped around Mirta and kept chattering away. I was very much in love with the way Mirta listened.

"If only there was a way we could bring all of this home with us . . . . "

"There are always souvenirs."

"Yes, but I don't want a baby crocodile. I want this productivity. I want Cuban shopping centers, Cuban supermarkets, Cuban automobile plants, Cuban products advertised on every free wall in the 'free world.' There's no eternal law barring us from having all of this. Havana can be Miami!"

"Let's hope not."

"In terms of aesthetics, I'll concur. But what about jobs? I must teach you to value employment over the picturesque. Let the Yankee children have their turn living in shacks. Let them flock to our cities, let them beg from us. Let them try to meet our 'standard of living,' let them learn to sing our songs. This is what your professors would call negation, no?"

"That's what they would call wishful thinking . . . . "

This was Mirta's only objection, though I went on raving about my new mistress instead of her. On a bus that crossed the causeway to Miami Beach, I stood on a broken rear seat and courted the U. S. of A.

"America, I know the joy of a smooth highway. . . America, I blow smoke rings, too. . . America, you are a stadium I could pack. . . America, you do not know how American I am!"

I don't think America understood my Spanish. The bus driver glared, the old women hardly peered out at me from behind the shopping bags in their laps, as if they'd seen hundreds frothing over like me, as though I was one more of those unbalanced souls who are yet another specialty of American production.

What may have driven me mad were the miniature golf courses. In Miami, they are works of genius: metal storks to swallow the balls, Dutch windmill hazards to sweep them up, whirlpools in the water traps, putting greens laid in purple plastic with slopes shaped like breasts, the holes positioned like nipples. Mirta hardly knew which end of the club to grip but I made her play game after game. I kept score, and though it pained me, I added strokes to my column, giving up par to keep Mirta close.

Finally, she insisted we spend some time on the beach. But how to get there? It was like being back in Cuba, where every square inch of the waterfront had been parceled out, where even the ocean was hoarded. I recollect searching for an alley between hotel pools, then scanning the bathers to find our own kind. Light to dark, rare to well-done, this rotisserie was strictly color-coded. I got so enraged that Mirta immediately led me into the water. That was her first mistake. The next was a challenge to show her my champion's form. I wanted so badly to exhibit my powers, my untapped strength. I wanted to remind myself that these Yankee waters were no different than our own. I could cleave them confidently. I could stay afloat here too. Before I surfaced for my first breath, I had swum far away from my wife. And then I kept going, kept heading out. Maybe I could make it all the way home. Maybe I could execute yet another daring getaway. But what predicament was I escaping from this time? I repeated my breaststroke until I was too exhausted for answers.

An hour must have passed before I came ashore. I landed at a private beach where guards quickly told me to move along. Stumbling back in my polka-dot trunks, shaking off the chill of deep waters, I convinced myself that I

was engaged in another of my pranks. That's it—I was trying to give Mirta a good laugh. Creeping up behind her,
I saw she was wrapped—no, collapsed—in our only beach
towel, her widow's shawl. She was trembling so hard that
she was moving in a dozen directions while standing quite
still. Beyond her, at the shoreline, a team of blond lifeguards did a jig in the riptides, gripping red emergency
floats. I didn't want to believe they were looking for me.

"Mmmmmirta... over here! You can find me! It's
easy!"

The problem was finding her. Spinning around, my
wife presented a face so uncharacteristically overwrought
that I wondered if she did not belong to some other
swimmer. The composure that was her best feature had
been erased with worry. Poor *abandonada*, in her black
one-piece! She latched onto me with ferocity. Her embrace
was a restraint, keeping me from ever leaving. She didn't
say a word. She made no signal to the lifeguards, just let
them go on searching.

PAUSE: DEATH IS THE ULTIMATE FORM OF PROPAGANDA
Did this really occur? It must have, because I'm wincing.
Yet for all my running away, I did not know how to be a
deserter. For all Mirta's clinging, she did not know how to
be loyal. For five years, we would try to be what we could
not be.

Upon our return to Havana, I set up a law firm, Mirta
set up a home. Like my father, I could have easily slept
and eaten right in my office. I had some difficulty adjust-
ing to a "private residence." I made certain my wife had
her difficulties too. I insisted she take the first apartment
we saw, a rotten Vedado walk-up, right on a noisy bus
route, with bad plumbing and green concrete walls. I did
not want Mirta to make a fuss over our personal comforts,

our hideout. Make a fuss! I wouldn't let her buy a dinette set from Sears or a matching china service for two. The days of high society were over. She was a struggling lawyer's spouse now. And I exacerbated the struggle by taking on cases without fees. I represented striking garbage collectors, distraught pensioners, persecuted writers. As in school, I rated an "outstanding" in labor law but only a "pass" in property. The few *pesos* I took in quickly went out again to a host of good causes. More often than not, I was paid in reputation. Mirta would have to prove her love by doing her shopping on that reputation. She was going to lead a life of sacrifice that I had not yet led myself.

Clearly, I was exhibiting serious deficiencies as a husband. I had more compassion for strangers than I did for Mirta. I took responsibility for unknown millions, but would not be responsible for the one who presented herself to be known. I was comfortable performing in a full auditorium, but I could not perform in the intimate arena. Yet from the moment we were engaged, Mirta appeared to humbly accept my growing indifference, the way the *campesinos* used to accept their winter's ration of dried black beans. What happened to her intoxicating resistance? Why did she have to surrender so fast? If she'd taken a stand, forced a "principled split," then we might have forged a principled front. But she never complained, she never castigated.

She did not question my devotion to her nor my capacity to become the leader of our people. No, she believed in both too much. But just as she came to view my love for her as one ambition too readily realized, so she saw my love for the people as yet another expression of my drive, even deviousness. She could not accept my activism as anything but a ploy. She refused to admit that the public man was the only man I was.

On our way home from some tedious rally, she would kiss me on the forehead, then whisper with a blackmailer's glee, "I know your secret." I would pretend I hadn't heard. If Mirta's only consolation was to be "in on the secret," I wasn't going to be the one to tell her that there was no secret.

Mirta remained faithful to me for all the wrong reasons. Yet the more misguided I knew her faith to be, the more I coveted it. I cherished her for all the wrong reasons, too. I was stupidly proud of my wife's background, of her regal dreaminess and upturned nose, her un-Cuban paleness, her lack of association with anything coarse. This girl who was going to "bring out the best in me" brought out the bourgeois in both of us.

Is that what compelled me to give her a child? No, I can't blame her entirely. I must be forthright. I wanted an heir.

"But what inheritance can you give him?" That was Raúl's question, while we played one-on-one basketball at the university gym.

I posted him down low, drove on him at will.

"His inheritance? Whatever it is, I shall give it to him freely, without conditions. . . " I wanted to be a father unlike any other, a champion father, unlike my own.

Raúl labled such a goal "reactionary." That was his favorite word at the time.

"But how can the propagation of the species be a reactionary act?"

Raúl answered me with his two-handed set shot. Deadly.

"We have many duties before us. We do not have the duty to breed . . . ."

My little brother had just joined the Communist Party. He was passing through that insufferable phase when the proletariat itself is not proletarian enough. And what phase was I passing through? Was I quietly tracking Raúl, blotting out his footprints with my larger ones?

The Yankee historians have always made a great issue of this. They're not scholars, they're policemen. They want every good "red" to register with them promptly, to kindly inform them as to the very moment at which they attained their redness. "And when did you start hating your boss? Or your mother?" As if we know! As if we are bound to recall the details of our premeditated crime! Or is it that they want us to paint bright bull's-eyes on our chests to facilitate the hunt? I wish the other side were so willing to identify themselves. If every capitalist stood up and proclaimed himself a proud exploiter, a self-conscious profiteer, a dedicated usurer, there wouldn't be any of them left on the planet.

How could I have been a communist when I scorned those doctrinaire pedants who called themselves Communists? I might have been. Was I a communist when Cuba's hand-me-down McCarthyites were calling everyone a communist? I had to be. Was I a communist when my enemies accused me of being a "Creole Stalinist"? Probably not, since I still don't know what that means.

Was I a communist when I immersed myself in legalism? When I pleaded for a new order to be imposed by writ? When I invoked justice before fattened, indifferent magistrates?

Was I a communist when I rose to the side of my idol, Eddy Chibás? When I was his good protégé and his bad bodyguard? Waiting outside the radio booth as he delivered the most stirring appeal of his Presidential campaign, I saw Chibás take the revolver from his coat pocket and shove the muzzle into his belly. I heard the shots and the sound of his spectacles smashing against the microphone.

I cradled Eddy Chibás in my bouncer's arm. I learned for the first time that death is the ultimate form of propaganda. Could I have been a communist then?

Could I have been a communist when I asked the struggle to take a short pause, to please not erupt, to keep quiet after ten at night, so my newborn could sleep? When I did not want my child to be disturbed and forgot about all the children who were already disturbed?

At this point in the recording, I will insert riotous applause, or, more appropriately, jeers.

If I was a communist, then I was one only in the sense of the slogan that became popular among our people in '61, when they needed to explain why their revolution had taken two years to call itself "communist." The people said, "The baby was born, but it had not been named . . . ."

As for our baby, Mirta and I had no trouble naming it. Ay, Fidelito! Son among so many true sons! How I wanted to guide him! How I wanted to be his commander-in-chief! But I couldn't even find him on the night of his birth. I'd been addressing the leaders of a bus drivers' strike, and when I came home, Mirta was gone. I searched all the city hospitals, but Mirta's parents had taken her to a private sanitarium. I had to enlist the aid of the police to find my namesake. Once I was led to his crib, I handled him too roughly. From the start, I made Fidelito cry. I did not find this distressing. When I held him, I was not holding a son, I was holding a model. His hunger was Cuba's hunger. His cries were Cuba's cries.

Somehow I could placate Cuba but I was never able to placate my son. He was too much mine, too like a possession. At the same time, he was so very ordinary. The son who trailed behind mamma and pappa: it was easy for him to march in that typical alignment, tougher for me. Yet I craved to be typical. And I'm not speaking of appearances here, I'm not referring to some illusion of stability required of a novice politician. I mean that I was still hoping to find out what it felt like to be stuck with simple, common emotions, to remain mired in humanity and held back from my historic task. I had no more success than I did when I was a boy. I treated that ordinary family most extraordinarily. I was constantly preoccupied with urgent business, just as my father had been preoccupied. I would boast to my colleagues about Fidelito's ample weight, his Castro appetite, but I was never there to feed him.

I did not like to do what was expected of me. The more that was expected, the more likely I was to be somewhere else.

I could not restrain myself from doing what was right, even if it hurt the good people around me.

I could not bear anonymity.

In theory, I did not have the makings of a model socialist. In theory, I was a swine.

Luckily, life confounds theory.

What confounded my plans, toppled my nest, was Batista's *coup*. It happened while Cuba and I slept, before I'd learned to keep my insomniac's guard. Since he knew he could not win the elections of 1953, the squat colonel, the strutting magpie, took control of the army at Camp Columbia and cancelled those elections. In the morning, at the bar where I took my *buchito*, my "little swallow" of coffee, I learned that I was no longer a candidate for Congress. All "respectable opposition" had been eliminated, and with it, my hopes of becoming the respectable lawyer or the respectable patriarch.

Which explains why Fidelito turned out the way he did. No, I shouldn't put it so negatively. He always chides me for being too critical. He says I have no right to be shocked that the influence of his mother has been so strong upon his nature. He did not care about her beliefs, only that she was his mother. That's what I hate about the isolated constituency called family: every child is burdened with allegiances, every child creates his own right and left wings.

Fidelito remembers his mother from a time when she could do no wrong. He does not remember me. When I should have been bringing him toys, I was toying with the assault on the Moncada garrison. I could not buy him his very own six-shooter because I had to buy my own M-1 rifle. I could not get him new clothes because I spent all I had on my general's uniform. When the tailor delivered it to me at the Siboney Farm, on the eve of our fearless attack, I was furious. It was at least three sizes too large. How could I lead my men into battle when I tripped on my cuffs?

I met those men, and a few exceptional women, at the Santamarías' apartment near O St. and 25th. I would tell Fidelito I was going there to play dominoes with his mysterious "uncles." And really, it was a kind of clubhouse for my latest gang. Today the gang meets in the chambers of state. Those unfamiliar faces, whiskerless and drawn, that crowded in upon me in the darkened kitchen as I sat atop a two-burner stove, plotting our first raid, are now stubbled and puffy with responsibility, familiar to all as Cuba's Central Committee. Gathered around me were a generation of leaders but they did not look like a generation that was going to amount to much: younger than I, less driven and also less corruptible, most of the Moncada recruits were "late bloomers," disenchanted students who'd graduated to mindless desk jobs. Human time bombs, they ticked off in bleak personnel bureaus, as accountants, as meek male secretaries, working mostly for North American firms.

Abel Santamaría worked for General Motors, Pontiac Division. He wore buttoned-down shirts, usually plaid. He wore tortoise shell glasses. He was a fanatic when it came to Vivaldi. Cuba came next. His chiseled chin jutted out as if about to be punched. It was a chin made for *bas relief*, for monuments. That was the only fault of this crowd, if they had any: they were a little too willing to die.

Without prompting, they sold their cars and their matching love seats, mortgaged their modest inheritances. They lined up for weapons as the devout line up for the Eucharist wafer. They got themselves readmitted to the university so they could use the shooting range. They never had to be cajoled or exhorted. They did not show a need to explain themselves either. In the midst of a conspiracy, as in the midst of lovemaking, reasons only get in the way.

They also knew how to keep their mouths shut. They kept the first secret in the history of the republic. After Renato purchased the red farmhouse in Siboney, on the outskirts of Santiago and its Moncada garrison, we pretended we were chicken farmers. To the farm we sent packets of ammo marked "chicken feed." I was the only one that knew who was going to eat those bullets. My soldiers arrived at Siboney posing as celebrants on the eve of Santiago's carnival. They shared the farm's one room as boarders. No one suspected them. Mirta did not suspect me. All she knew was that I was driving to Santiago "on business." She also knew that I might not return for some months and that this prospect made me unusually sanguine.

"Tell the boy I have gone to get him the best present a father can give!"

"But will I hear from you?"

"You may hear about me."

"And when will you return?"

"When I have run out of secrets. . . ."

Driving east across the island this time, back to Oriente, I hoped the old DeSoto could make it. "Fidel's Bus" remained empty. I couldn't take chances with hitchhikers. I was convinced that I was steering toward victory or death. The record shows that I arrived at neither. Instead, I would become the mouthpiece of martyrs. I would clean up after a systematic slaughter of my captured troops which was too cruel to have been anticipated or imagined. For all the tirades I hurled against the dictator, for all of my years of outrage, I still had not properly gauged the enemy's vileness. My perceptions were tainted by empathy. As I reached the blue mountains that circle Santiago, I thought of how lonely Batista must feel, lonely in his palace, poor boy. I troubled myself over the shock I knew he would feel at the news of our plot. I commiserated with the generals I hoped to frustrate. I reminded myself to send telegrams of consolation to the mothers of all the guards we would kill. I was trying to have mercy for all sides while striking a blow for only one. Forget it. You don't win a war by putting yourself in the spot where you shoot. In underestimating Colonel Fulgencio's gusto for killing, I was underestimating the threat we posed.

I was supposed to spend the night at an apartment near Parque Céspedes. But do you think I could sleep then when I can't sleep now? I roamed the streets until dawn. I left the message that I was staking out our target, that I was plotting last-minute adjustments in our strategy. Actually, I joined Santiago's carnival revelers. I didn't have to worry about being identified because everyone was wearing a mask. Mine was solid black, so that I looked like a court jester in a shabby grey suit. No one could have guessed what I was up to. What omniscience! What delectable mastery! I was lost amidst the people.

Whole neighborhoods did the cha-cha through Santiago's cobblestone maze and I stutter-stepped along. Santiago, shrine of Oriente, "cradle of rebellion," home to all things and beings truly Cuban! Santiago, imperfect pearl, tilework tongue set in a throat of azure bay. Santiago, *muy linda*. Still courtyards, banana leaves, rumors. City of faces, craggy and imperturbable. Santiago, scented with the rum of the Bacardis, drenched in conspiracy. Here, when I was sent to stay with relatives, I had wet my bed at the sound of gunfire in the back alleys from the doomed rebellion of '33. Now it was '53 and these alleys were swollen with song, with congas and *timbales* and tin cans struck like cymbals. Tomorrow there would be gunfire in Santiago again.

Tomorrow I might be dead. So what? The fear of death was of consequence only because it kept all life in place. Once that threat, that excuse, was removed, the time-cards of our nation would stop being punched; the churches would empty; the jails would fly open. Everything that was unjust would be at stake. Take away the fear of death and what was left? Only the carnival, swirling around me.

Besides, "Dying is an easy thing compared to living." That's what Abel Santamaría told me when I reached the farmhouse on the morning of July 26. Poor Abel! Thanks to a Cain named Fidel, he would soon have a chance to prove his point. He wanted to be at the head of the charge. At Siboney, we fought to save one another.

"You must not expose yourself, Alejandro. You must not throw your mantle away senselessly, like Martí ...."

"No Abel, you must be there if I am cut down. I may be the movement's nerve center, its whip. But you, you are its soul!"

We were not showing much confidence in our plan. In the end, I made it an issue of rank. I ordered Abel to stay out of harm by securing a nearby hospital. His sister

Haydée and a doctor would be his regiment. Then I out-
lined the full scheme to the rest of the men. For the first
time, I made them aware of the exact dimensions of our
daring. With my orders, I also gave them a last chance to
refuse. None did. The sun was rising faster than it ever
had. There was time only for the briefest of remarks and a
large glass of milk per man.

Moncada proved a splendid disaster, the blunder of
which we could all be proud. What had Pedrito said to me
on the Candy Key? "Mistakes are advantages in disguise."
Only when so many things went wrong could we glimpse
what might happen when they went right. The armory we
captured to procure more arms turned out to be the barracks' barber shop. The second car, carrying crucial reinforcements for the surprise attack, took a wrong turn just
before the guard house. The uprising had begun, shots
were being fired, the Moncada's pitiful limestone turrets
were in sight—and this driver was lost, this Chevrolet was
cruising in circles! If we'd had a grenade or two, this bit of
misdirection would not have mattered. We were just
entering the seminary of war, where the teacher is always
trial and error. But why so many trials, so many errors?
Abel was waiting at the hospital, where I'd dispatched him
to prepare for the humane treatment of the wounded,
where I was certain he'd be safe. But that hospital became
the most dangerous of combat zones; the treatment he
would receive was hardly humane. Isolated from our with-
drawal, Abel disguised himself as a patient. When a pal-
sied informant pointed him out, Abel's false bandages
were stripped away, his wounds were made real.

"In death, life begins." Martí was right, but being right
is not always a consolation. In her holding cell, Haydée Santamaría was brought the severed testicles of her
brother.

Our struggle, our island, has been small enough to insure an intimacy about combatants. There is no Cuban "unknown soldier." In this Revolution, the martyrs were always friends, friends of friends, friends of lovers. I can never lose track of these interdependencies, of the direct links between our living and our dead. From the crowded kiosks of La Rampa to the smallest cluster of *bohíos*, the informal commemoration goes twenty-four hours, one industry we don't have to modernize. Wherever I take my government in a jeep, I am reminded of what I already know: that I sent so many breathing things to their deaths. My least favorite contradiction is that I had to build my whole strategy on the people's natural aptitude for sacrifice when so many of those people—their faces, their talents, their motives—were known to me personally.

How was it that I did not share their fate? Why did they fall around me but never on me? It is said that I have led a charmed existence. I say that charm has no material basis. I would rather credit the wearing of our movement's "moral vest." It's too hot in the tropics to wear the bulletproof kind! Where virtue puts a man in danger, virtue must be what gets him out.

After the Moncada debacle, I ran for the hills. Where else? Again, I padded through the underbrush, dodged the thin and nearly leafless hardwoods, swept the vines from my eyes and tore the thorny *mamoncillos* from my ankles, felt the moist earth give beneath the demands of my flight, sought the high ground that shelters all ideals. Batista ordered his men to bring Fidel Castro out of the Sierra Maestra as a corpse. But the young lieutenant who caught up with me was none other than Sarría, a former classmate at the university. He was a poor student who had once asked me to write a portion of his philosophy exam. I never refused to undertake such favors though I had no idea how useful this one would prove. No, I had simply treated Sarría as I treated anyone in need. In return, here he was, warning me not to give my right name, concealing my identity from the rest of the search party until I was safely in public view.

Years later, in the mountains once more, a Judas infiltrated our original guerrilla unit. Eutimio Guerra, a sad name. We began to suspect him when he talked about his dreams each morning over the campfire. Who else could be bothered with such concerns? Yet each time Eutimio would dream of some calamity, it happened. Che was the first to suggest that this was Eutimio's manner of confession: "We endorse the right to dream, Fidel, but we condemn the right to premonition." By the time the traitor woke with the prediction of my death, we knew he was plotting it. He went over the hill for supplies and came back with a concealed knife. Yet he was so intent on his mission that he'd left his overcoat in town. With a wink at Che, I offered to share my blanket with the assassin. All night we lay huddled together like two Boy Scouts. I don't think Eutimio had any dreams. I don't think he slept. For a change, I slept blissfully. I had taken pity on him and felt certain he would take pity on me. Though he held the blade an inch from my heart, though I snuggled ever closer, daring him on, I knew he would not do the deed. In the morning, we shot Eutimio Guerra. Kneeling before Che's pistol, he made us promise to treat his children as good citizens of the revolution. We have.

To thwart my attackers, I embraced them. Before they could thank me for my gracious welcome, I gobbled them up. Isn't that how an anti-body works on a germ? Nature provides all the models. Lose touch with its wellsprings, you lose touch with your own. To the hills, always! But don't go there to hide, go there to be forthright! It was my love for wild and uncharted places—including the open *plaza* and the expanse of outfield grass—that confounded so many plots against my life. I will not relinquish a moment of sunlight. That's why the *bonches* failed, why the National Guard was frustrated, why the C.I.A. could not get at me with their underworld henchmen and their exploding *cigarillos*. These predators strike in alleys and well-secured conference rooms. They're insulted by targets that are so appallingly easy to hit.

But where was I? Often, it seems that I speak in one vast digression, that my locution is circumlocution—and that my life is a series of connected detours I am compelled to take so I'm made aware of the route from which I've strayed. It is the unswerving pathway of one who survives.

PAUSE: A LITTLE TIME AND A LOT OF INK

For the Moncada survivors, life went on, cruel and sordid as ever. What kind of life was this when we found our highest compliment in the enemy's ruthlessness? What kind of world was this where we could begin to take ourselves seriously only when we saw that we could provoke fear? In that moment when I took myself most seriously, I got my big chance. Pleading the case of our movement before the nation's high court, I had finally reached center stage. The part designated for me was one for which I'd been training since I'd leafed through my first accounts of the American Revolution, since my first appeals before my father's bench. No wonder I felt so at ease! I was not merely an imitation of Patrick Henry, bereft of wig. I was not just Danton, not just another *La Pasionaria*. I had become me, an advocate for my right to exist. I never had such an easy defense. I will never again orate with such legal precision. Being led to the docket, I was still correcting my script. "History will forgive me"? Too contrite. "History will bless me"? Too precious. "History will soothe me"? Too lurid. "History will succor me"? Too much. "History will use me, disabuse me .... History will dissolve me." No. *"History will absolve me!"*

Despite the millions of words credited to me, these four are my theology. I could not have believed in history if I were a Catholic; I could not have believed in absolution if I weren't.

But would Mirta absolve me? I wasn't asking. My first message to her was that she should print two hundred thousand copies of my speech. She wrote back that there was money enough to print two hundred. I wrote her that the only difference between two hundred and two hundred thousand was a little time and a lot of ink.

I knew that prison would be a rich experience, from which I would gain an acuity and fortitude beyond measure. Everyone can use a good humbling, a good flogging now and then—except those who are permanently humbled, perpetually flogged. Besides, where else but prison could a man like me be forced to take a rest? I have always been so impervious to punishment that I brought it down on myself. I was disappointed when I found out how comfortable a jail cell could be. In time I would fill mine with a library of nineteenth century European literature alongside a stockpile of gourmet hams and canned pineapple rings. What kind of martyrdom was this? Through all my tests, I suspected that I was somehow untested, untried. Despite my fearsome bent for sacrifice, I wound up being coddled. I was always the boy born to get what he pleased.

Which is not to say that I was pleased by captivity. In those first months, before I was transferred from solitary confinement, I could not stand up to the torture of silence. My defense was to hold conversations with the only company I was afforded: the rotting carcasses of my compatriots, left in the prison corridor. "How was that last glass of milk I gave you, Renato? Did you feel its beneficial effects as you sprinted toward annihilation? I could use some complete protein right now . . . . Don't laugh. Nutrition is the building block of revolution. Do you know what the best staple would be for a poor country like ours? Seafood! And it's all around us! Instead, we scrounge for beans . . . . I've been studying such matters, to be ready when we take charge . . . . What's that? You'd like me to study your fist? Be careful, *hombre*. I'm still twice your size. I only look short because I have to stoop when I stand in this cage." I don't believe I defiled my partners by using them in this way. Their memories were already beyond defilement. And I'm quite sure I did not reveal any valuable information, except that Fidel Castro likes to talk, that Fidel Castro does not enjoy being alone. It was not that I was unwilling to confront myself. It was just that I could not bear being removed from the ongoing Cuban cacophony.

I had to develop patience the way I'd once developed my biceps. I began following a strict schedule by which I reduced the hours for fuming. The only time I fell apart was when I was allowed to see Fidelito. A little boy in short pants, skipping through a dungeon trying to find his old man. He was a part of me on the loose—with my wavy hair, my longing eyes and weak, rounded chin. For his sake, the authorities had removed the corpses. Very thoughtful, except now Fidelito wanted to know where all my friends were. What had happened to the many "uncles" who had brought him presents while they were bringing me guns and maps and their hearts? I lied to my son. I don't believe that I have done so since but what could I tell him? "Boris is hacked to pieces, Juan is another exhibit for the museum of mutilation, Abel was not treated according to the Geneva Code." I wept when my boy left me. I would have wept harder had I known I would not see him again for six years.

If my men had heard me, they would have thought I was being tortured, and I was, most effectively. The worst tortures are always self-inflicted, no? I learned this from that little boy's mother. I was counting on Mirta to carry out each assignment smuggled to her. I trusted her to coordinate the work of the July 26 Movement, though she was only a member *ex officio*. I did not concern myself with her personal convictions, nor did I consider how she and the boy would be fed. Then I read a newspaper headline: "Castro Wife on Government Stipend." The article said that her brother Rafael, now working for the Ministry of Interior, had arranged to pay Mirta a salary for some fraudulent job. I refused to believe she would accept such unseemly aid. Her signature on those checks was undoubtedly forged. I turned to the sports page, unruffled by such slander. I wrote to Mirta, pledging my unequivocal support.

My pledge came too late. I should have known that my wife would not straggle behind me no matter where I roamed. I should have known she would not stain the hem of her white dress with the guava green of the gutter. How could I have counted on Mirta's fidelity when it had always been such an incongruous gift? My assumptions had nothing to do with the vagaries of romance and everything to do with the debts of matrimony. Though I'd hardly been much of a husband, I expected her to be wifely unto eternity. In my battle against tradition, I had counted on this one tradition being upheld. It was my turn to be surprised, to be left on the beach.

First, Mirta admitted she'd been supported by the dictatorship. I was tainted, discredited, stunned. Next, my sister Lidia brought me papers to sign. Mirta was filing for divorce.

I nearly strangled Lidia for bearing the news. Then I gave her a speech:

"Every true emotion is a repeated emotion. It has been experienced by every member of the species and therefore cannot be entirely foreign. It is already part of us and we are prepared. Strange as it may sound, I believe that human beings would be discouraged if the worst did not occasionally occur."

The moment Lidia left me alone, I lost hold of such a dispassionate view. I slumped to my cot and went into a pure *machismo* stupor. Who knows how long it lasted? The cell, like my heart, had no clock. Though I had not permitted myself to wallow in the losses sustained at Moncada, I found it highly permissible to wallow in the loss of my manhood. Though I should have predicted my wife's treacherous return to the elitist fold, I could not forgive her lack of discretion. On the prison ceiling, I pictured the masses' one big cyclops eye and cursed Mirta for letting that eye in on our marriage. It was in our bedroom, it was measuring my organ's length. It had seen me cuckolded, morally and politically. I could hear all Cuba asking, "How can he seize the reins of power when he does not have the power to keep a rein on his wife?"

Notice: I did not give the masses credit for being able to make the distinction between these two realms of power. But it was I who could not make it, particularly when word reached me that Mirta was engaged to marry the son of Batista's Ambassador to the United Nations. They were taking my son away from me, too. My Fidelito nursed by reactionaries, tucked in by apologists! This was bad opera. But now that the libretto of our divorce was written with politics in the mouths of the players, I had even less trouble telling the hero from the villains. I felt betrayed on all fronts.

And what was my heroic response? I wrote a letter to the newspapers threatening suicide. Yes, I would do the job myself, since most of the island seemed so eager for it to be done. The corpses of my comrades were now signposts that beckoned me. I wanted to join my friends, to see Abel and Eddy Chibás and *El Apóstol*. I wanted to look down from that pantheon and its invulnerability. I wanted to take out my membership in that brotherhood of harbingers. If I tried hard enough, I could reduce myself to another flash in the torrid Cuban pan. I could prove that I too was noble enough to be doomed. But what was so noble about having my wife be the cause?

I should have been thanking her for her liberating gift. Imprisoned, I was free. Stripped, I had everything I wanted. In my forced seclusion, I felt her presence more vividly than I ever had.

Ironies are never ironic in their moment of revelation. First, they are direct blows.

Eventually, a cushion is formed by the lessons we draw. We want so badly to be teachers when the best we can hope for is that we will be taught.

I began studying those lessons here, on the Isle of Pines, where the prison facilities included an actual classroom. In the setting that inspired Stevenson's "Treasure Island," I mined my own treasures. Reading fourteen hours a day, I did not restrict myself to political economy. I discovered the Russian novelists, plowing through the complete works of Dostoyevsky and Gorky. What incisiveness, what utter transcendence of one's own times! And I needed all the transcendence I could get. I reacquainted myself with the French pre-modernists, especially Balzac and Zola. How could we lose when hypocrisy was so mercilessly exposed? For amusement, I would skim Thackeray and Dickens while sunbathing on my porch and savoring the smooth *Upmanns* supplied by my followers. Thanks to sympathizers among the prison staff, I was equipped with my own hot plate. I could filter my coffee and create all sorts of delicacies. I made a respectable spaghetti in squid sauce. I was living better than I could in a suite at the Havana Hilton.

My chief duty was to prepare my weekly class for the Abel Santamaría School. I was the headmaster, you might say, Raúl the chief proctor. Here we were, hardened terrorists, kept alive only to mollify the regime's vague understanding of "public opinion," and we were busily dissecting Emile Durkheim and Edmund Burke. We discussed the symbolism involved in the plight of Jean Valjean. I acquainted the men with Max Weber's "charismatic man," making sure they did not think I was referring to myself! I drilled my soldiers in Aristotelian logic, in phenomenology and especially in ethics. There was nothing more effective for prison morale than to link our plight to the most ancient, the most elevated strivings. The more elevated and ancient, the better. I had one rule in my classroom: no current events.

However, an analysis of *Anna Karenina* led me to introduce the topic that was foremost in my concerns. Did I envision myself as the heartsick Karenin or the sicker Vronsky? In either case, I could not help asking the men, "When we romanticize an event or an endeavor or a woman, what are we really doing?" An answer came swiftly. These were quick learners. "When we adore something we are also obscuring it. We are seeing what we would wish to see." The class had concluded that the woman we celebrate in song, or bestow with roses, was no woman at all but rather a reflection of our own conceit. The woman who could be as angry as we were, as awkward, as foolish, and as brutal, was the woman we had to value.

I had given up hope of ever finding such a woman. Courtship, always tortuous, now seemed impossible. When you have become El Jefe Máximo, you cannot cast moon eyes at every young article. But then you came along, Celia . . . well, I don't want to make this sound like a swimsuit competition. And I don't know why I have made you wait so long to hear about what my first love did to me.

Is there so much to tell? Is it any shock to you that I have not led the most exemplary of lives? Why can't I accept my imperfections the way I accepted yours?

If you could just see me now, Celia, leaning back in my cast-iron chair, feet on the table, bunions making my socks bulge. Pulling out my green shirttails, I see too much fat around the waist, plenty of purposeless hair and pockmarks beneath. On the table, pinned down by the recorder, I see forms, requisitions, urgent requests from Soviet traders and disgruntled pensioners, errors to erase, orders to countermand, misunderstandings and misapplications to mediate. One thing I don't see is perfection.

Again, love and revolution are analogous: neither can survive on a pedestal. In my closing lecture to the men I recalled "the spoiled limbs of our compatriots, turning blue and bored through with maggots." I had asked, "Were those martyrs meant for perfection?" I had heard the answer, "They were meant to be men."

The mind of man moves whole galaxies, his arms and legs shove one boulder at a time. My followers and I may have been enraptured with our talk but we were still in chains. From then on, we had to honor every misstep, wrest visions from our blindness, go forward with a confidence that belongs only to clowns.

Released from prison in the amnesty of '55, all I had to do was leave Cuba for Mexico, mount my invasion, return with "the dictator beheaded at my feet." That's what I said and what the history books record. They tell how I stood at the prison gate, thanking our keepers for their subversive kindness. They don't tell how I scanned the crowds at the gate hoping Mirta and Fidelito would be there to greet me. They depict the tumultuous scene at my sister's house in Havana, so packed with well-wishers that my *guayabera* was shredded as I fought my dismay at the absence of my wife and son from the guest list. Setting out on my most taxing climb, I was weighed down with remorse. At each campsite, I pitched the tent of my personal tragedy. Just when I needed all my renowned vigor, I was sapped by an individualist fever. I was infected with the virus of loneliness.

My fabled invasion was in no healthier condition. Our training grounds outside Mexico City were raided. Our troops were hounded by spies. Often we did not have enough money for *frijoles*, let alone guns. But it was more than hunger that inspired me to keep issuing proclamations and threats that looked harder and harder to enforce. I was goading myself on, going through the motions until my mission was made manifest to me. I had not lost my nerve. I never lost that. But I feared that this brashness had become my sole claim to leadership. Though I had moved from politician to prophet, leading my ragtag flock toward some promised land, I could sense that I was still speaking and swaggering like one of a hundred hot-blooded, short-fused nationalists. My sincerity—the only currency that bought my mercenaries—was becoming devalued.

I went north of the border on fundraising tours. I accepted contributions from the most disreputable business interests, telling them whatever they wanted to hear about the July 26 Movement's program. These homesick *Habaneros* did not want to hear about ideology. They wanted to see me wave the flag: "Let us stand up and sing the immortal hymn whose verses say that to live in chains is to live under shame and insult, while to die for the fatherland is to live!" As the hat was passed, I would harp on our poverty: "We all live modestly. Each of our men in exile sustains himself with far less than the cost of a horse to the army. None of us will ever be seen in a nightclub or bar. The first revolutionary manifesto was printed with money from a pawned overcoat ... " There was no need for exaggeration. Nor did I lie at the Palm Gardens in *Nueva York*, when I told an assembly of bookmakers and merchants: "I do not live in a particular place. I reside somewhere in the Caribbean and can feel as much at home in a city like this one as on a barren and deserted little island ...."

New York! I did not dare admit just how at home I felt there. I wanted to see the Yankees play ball. I wanted to gape at Wall Street. I wanted to ride back and forth all night on the Staten Island Ferry. It was in New York that Mirta and I had spent our happiest times. We had gone there shortly after the honeymoon, at the expense of her parents, who were encouraging me to attend the Law School at Columbia. I never had any intention of going there but I did intend to spend all of the Díaz Balarts' money. I showed Mirta the town as if I was a native. I took her to restaurants I had read about in *Pal Joey*. It made no difference that we were staying in a dirty tenement corseted with fire escapes. If my memory is still trustworthy, this apartment was amidst the cockroaches of West 82nd Street, not a great distance from the Hotel Theresa, my headquarters when I first spoke to the U.N. I would bring more chickens with me that next time, and less cash. If I recall correctly, Mirta and I also visited Central Park Zoo. It was there, on my next visit, that I had an urge to climb into the lions' cage. I felt trapped by the cordon of police and cameramen and secret agents all around me. Quickly, I hoisted myself over the bars. *Voila!* New York had never seen a head of state so agile. The lions snoozed in their asphalt lair. They didn't care who I was. In their company, I was set free. From my new vantage point, I could see that my captors had been captured. They were frozen. All those self-appointed protectors were powerless to protect me from myself.

That was what this city did to me. Such a concentration of power seemed to titillate me, to shake me up like one of those subway trains. It was always inspiring to know what I was up against. It was always enthralling to come courting my illicit "Empire State" lover.

In '55, vulnerable to seduction, I actually contemplated an elopement. Staying at the homes of supporters in Union City, New Jersey, I spent a dreadful night resisting the temptation to disappear. What was luring me away from the cause? I remember only the silhouettes of oil drums, and traffic lights blinking for no one. I remember that I had another good tussle with my old friend, the voice of despair in his derby hat.

"Add it up right, Fidel!" the voice admonished. "Who's against you? Practically everyone you have ever known. Who's for you? Mostly those you will never know." He was very persuasive. "You are only twenty-eight. Why die now? For what? An idea? You could wake up tomorrow with an entirely new one. Don't be the noble schoolboy forever, don't be a big fish in a puddle of spit. A man with your initiative would be properly appreciated in the United States. He wouldn't be punished or hunted down the way you are by your ungrateful countrymen. Put some Coke in your rum and be done with it. You could find a new wife here too . . . ."

I ended up running only so far as the nearest telephone booth. Struggling with my English, I asked the operator for the number of the U.N. Ambassador, now the father-in-law of my wife. But what would I say to him, or to Mirta if he led me to her? "Tell me, what's it like living only for one's self? Are you happy, *corazón?* . . . Do you keep a secret scrapbook of my clippings? Do you still know how to keep that white dress clean?"

And I'd still like to know: "How was it, Mirta Díaz Balart, that you were the only adversary who ever left me ambushed? How did you catch me so defenseless when you must have thought my defenses were impenetrable? Can you sketch the battle maneuvers, the weapons utilized, the territory in dispute? Did you keep a record in a diary, like Che?"

Don't worry. I won't send an agent to confiscate it, or get some Russian satellite to photograph your wrinkles. Only the powerful are required to grow blubbery before the world. Only the great are held accountable for their dead ends.

That sudden end, that lack of completion is what haunted me, what made me remember my wife and made me try to forget. But what sort of resolution was I after? Could I have demanded custody of our son so that he could learn to throw grenades or serve as the brigade water boy? What I really wanted was to hear Mirta beg my forgiveness. Or did I want her to forgive me? Emotions that are irrational also tend to be interchangeable. In any case, I did not telephone anyone because I had already used my last dime.

Episodes like these remind me that while the historic

process is inexorable, an individual's place in that process may be determined through several critical moments of pure choice. Can I find half the locations where a wrong turn would have led me forever astray from the revolution's broad highway? How did I find my bearings? What was my road map? I would like to think it was the writings of Carlos Marx but I must concede that I came to them much too late. They would serve as a kind of grand atlas on which I could superimpose my already worn navigational charts. No, I was kept on track by a Galician stubbornness, by an Oriente recklessness, by a landowner's arrogance, by a bully's confidence, by a bastard's detachment. Distasteful as it may be, I must finally give my upbringing its due.

I could also give it to other people. After all, I was not going through all these crises by myself. I was committed to the rescue of others, so they rescued me. If you want something badly enough, someone is bound to provide it. The permutations of probability make it likely: there are so many of us, so many productive combinations. If you wish to be led astray, a man will point and you will be lost. If you wish to go forward, the same man will point in the very same direction and you will be found.

For me, that man was a vagrant who accosted Raúl in a Mexico City park. This one took snapshots of strollers with an old Kodak Brownie, then tried to foist off the results, begging payment against some future delivery. But he was not very good at his game. Short and barrel-chested, he had trouble keeping up with his random victims. A slow-talking Argentine, he had to further interrupt his halting sales pitch with gasps for breath and some not very saleable slobbering. When Raúl brushed him aside, the photographer confessed, "This is not the device I would like in my hands. These are not the subjects I would like to hold captive."

That was enough for my brother to buy the beggar a double *filtro.* Inside the cafe, Raúl was impressed by the stranger's frequent references to Gramsci and Rosa Luxemburg. He was astonished by the number of countries where this street artist had engaged in organizing work and by the number that had honored him with expulsion. Raúl was also sold on the man's honesty: the incompatibility of his fighting spirit and his obvious fraility, the chasm between his world-shattering goals and his ragamuffin appearance, could not have been easily fabricated. The only time Raúl doubted the stranger was when he claimed to be a doctor. If he was, so much the better.

We gathered what intelligence we could before inviting him to join us. We got good reports. The snapshot artist was indeed a doctor. Moreover, he was known to every group on the Mexican left: commanded by none, loyal to all. For the rest, we had to go on faith. And though this lack of reliable clearance guaranteed that we were regularly betrayed, it also guaranteed that our faith would be frequently and spectacularly rewarded. However, we did take the precaution of staging my first meeting with this volunteer far from our secret base, at the ranch-style adobe of a wealthy sympathizer in the volcanic suburbs of Lomas de Chapultepec.

I waited for the stranger in the study. To him, I must have looked like a banker: wearing a three-piece suit, necktie loosened, in an easy chair set before shelves of back-lit pre-Colombian figurines. It was not the impression I would have liked to give.Yet this man would one day write that he recognized me instantly as that rare, true adventurer, a man who took pleasure in risks. Now he is gone, having become the archetypal adventurer, the incessant risk-taker. This man saw in me what he wanted to see and I was pleased that he wanted so much.

When he first sat on the floor cross-legged, scorning a chair, packing his hand-whittled pipe and spilling strands of tobacco all over the white carpet, I could not see much in him. Or did I? The first time he looked up at me, I experienced a rare sensation. I was scared. Though he breathed laboriously, drooling off the end of the pipe from the effort of inhaling, I got the feeling I'd have to rip this man's vital organs apart one by one before his spirit could be subdued. When he reached into his satchel for a pocket knife, I nearly called my bodyguards. But he was soon applying the knife to an apple he'd brought along, wielding it with a surgeon's skill.

He was otherwise undistinguished. He affected no rakish beret in those days. I recall no red star. Instead, he wore a stained woolen poncho that obviously did double duty as his blanket. His vagabond's air made his age indeterminate, except that his lips were pursed with the sternness of outraged youth. Yet one could see that he was poor in a way that poor people never are. He began bragging to me about how little he'd had to eat in the past week. He lit a match and held it to his palm, hoping for applause. He flashed his dirty fingernails in my face, then scratched at a chin that had been shaved with a clam shell. His breath was wicked with chili peppers. And his feet! He did not contribute a good scent to our cause. Yet that smell was like camphor burned at a bug-infested campsite. This man was a flame who would scald the past out of me. He would disinfect everything.

"You are Ernesto Guevara?" I wanted him to think that this was not all we knew about him.

"That is the name on the passport issued by the country of my birth. Also, in the file of subversives. But I am called Che, especially by those who, like me, do not believe in countries . . . ."

"Then how do you expect to fight for ours?"

"Is your country so different from any other? Does it starve any better than the others? Does it require any more sacrifice? Does it ask for more than death?"

"No. But who knows? It may require life."

"I am ready even for that, though it may not look that way. I have been living like an animal only because I have not yet found the society of men."

He did not really have to tell me anything more. Yet Che went on to list his qualifications. "I can do more than doctoring. But I already know about treating the wounded of our continent. I have donated my skills to Peruvian farmers and thieves. I worked six months in a leprosarium. I am also handy with rifles and blades. I was taught to make rafts and pontoons by the Indians, in my younger days, when I played Huck Finn of the Amazon."

Now Che laughed for the first time but the laugh turned into a vicious asthmatic wheeze.

"I don't let this affliction stop me. I have worked in the copper mines, also as a mountain guide. I was a stevedore. And a soccer coach at a private academy, one of my triumphs. I was fired when I told the team they did not have to wear the school colors . . . ."

"And what else can you do?" I wasn't serious but I got a serious answer.

"I write poetry. And leaflets."

My only misgiving about this new recruit was that he might be dangerously self-sufficient. Types like this often thought they had nothing left to learn from other men. But he obviously needed another challenge, one more hurdle in the obstacle course he'd laid out for himself. I have often wondered what Che would have done if he'd been unable to find an outlet for his masochism—yes, his boundless masochism—in the Cuban cause. I suspect he would have died at the back of a one-*peso cantina*, in a resting place for those with scruples strict enough to insure degradation. Where would Che have met his end? In Bogotá or La Paz or Montevideo. It would not have made any difference to him if he'd been swept away in the gutters of Calcutta or the shanties of Capetown. But Che's martyrdom would then have been known only through word-of-mouth, his legend would have been recounted by angelic beggars and philosophers of the street.

Che and I tried not to talk philosophy at that first meeting. We had too much to do. No, it was only victory that enabled us to indulge that bent. Since I could not yet discuss the details of our invasion, we traded opinions on international relations. Che had some unkind words for the Organization of American States. He did not trust the intentions of old General "Ike" in Guatemala. He quoted from the Monroe Doctrine and the Communist Manifesto. Then he reached into his torn satchel for his favorite passages from Neruda and Heinrich Heine, read to me from leather-bound volumes. Che lugged this library wherever he went, even on our toughest climbs in the Sierra. He also carried a portable chess set at all times. When we ran out of food, ideas were his food. Che saw no division between ideas and acts. The acquisition of an idea *was* an act, the primary act. Culture was the primary battleground. And culture, for Che, was everything that exalted the simple human being.

That first night he asked me what I thought of Rimbaud, Dixieland jazz, the films of Luis Bunuel. I answered with what I'd memorized of the Gettysburg Address and the U.S. Army field manual for a sixteen-millimeter mortar.

At the time of our rendezvous, Che was more advanced in theoretical areas, while I was more advanced in the area of nasty invincibility. I had been a brawler for so long that I was a one-man battalion. Che was a one-man ambulance corps. In many ways, we were opposites, attracted like opposites. While I had been reared in the cane fields, Che was thoroughly urban, raised in an apartment building. While my parents were backward and pragmatic, Che's were progressive and stringently moral. While mine encouraged me with rebuffs, Che's encouraged him with a smile. Still, both of us had achieved our academic goals. Both of us had married and been fathers. Both of us had left careers and marriages behind. If we were different in ways that intrigued us, in ways that mattered we were alike. Overbearing relatives could not have made a better match.

Yes, Che and I were a perfect couple. I admit this. That night, we found a love at first sight. That comfortable adobe served as our honeymoon cottage. "In Lomas de Chapultepec. . . ." That almost sounds like the chorus of a newlyweds' serenade.

We talked the whole night, then went into the rock garden to watch the sun come up over slate cold Popacatépetl. To seal our match, we did not speak of love. We spoke of its opposite. This was Che's suggestion, an exercise he used often to replenish his venom. He told me, "The right to hate must be regained before we can regain the right to love." He said, "It is worse to feel shame at our distress than shame at our pleasures." He added, "Unhappiness is the poor man's only wealth, the poor nation's only renewable resource." He insisted, "We must learn to cherish our dissatisfactions."

So Che and I exchanged hates. I had to go first.

Fidel: "For one thing, I hate 'security.' We were not put on this earth to be secure. For another, I hate genuflection. I hate all forms of ancestor worship."

Che: "I hate peasants who sniff at a new dish set before them, but won't taste it."

Fidel: "I hate rosy young mothers, wheeling their prams, who dream only of their tots' brilliant futures and forget that the world isn't rosy, that there aren't enough brilliant futures to go around."

Che: "I hate buying on credit, middlemen, Chase Manhattan's briefcase killers."

Fidel: "I hate sweethearts, sick hearts, sad hearts."

Che: "I hate formal receptions, obligatory introductions and toasts, self-congratulation, servants bearing hors d'oeuvres."

Fidel: "I hate fawners and idolators and yes-men. And I hate lovers, those ultimate yes-men."

Che: "Protocol makes me puke."

Fidel: "I hate sore losers because I am one."

Che: "I hate straw bosses and border guards."

Fidel: "I hate slipping clutches, leaky washers, blown generators, this maintenance that saps us before we can go forward."

Che: "I hate informers."

Fidel: "I hate professors, those intellectual snitches, those policemen of ideas."

Che: "I hate the 'quest for peace,' Pentagon-style."

Fidel: "I hate everything that lacks substance, including joy."

Che: "I hate every notion that divides one person from another, including these hatreds of mine."

Fidel: "I hate regrets. If it were up to me, regrets would be punishable by death."

Che: "I hate wages. No matter how high the payment, there is no amount of cash equal to human effort given unwillingly."

Che again: "I hate the hysteria to be fed, found exclusively among those who have never been hungry."

Fidel: "I hate what poverty does to a people. I hate the

sight of our countless poor, who shuffle in slippers through a tropical stupor, who sweep their mud steps, pining for linoleum and pink dresses, who beat down their wishes with their laundry against washboards. Who, despite all our best intentions, remain victims, live lives without expression, without influence, without a fair shot at meaning."

Che: "I am not fond of money."

Fidel: "Above all else, I hate opinions: the expounding of opinions, the encounter of one opinion with another. Opinions are the real estate of thinking—everyone would like to invest in one, or better yet, squat upon it for life. But why bother to advance an idea if you are not willing to do all you can to implement it, including murder? Otherwise, you might as well be a stone."

Just ask Che. Che, Che! How lucky you are to be done with that exhausting, confounding dismay we both felt when faced with a world where greed was the rule and goodness the exception. One, two, many Ches . . . now there are Ches everywhere, but not the Che I need. How can I build the new man without your living blueprint? What counsel can you offer me from a poster?

He stares down at me now wherever I go, sanitized, the "prophet of love." I am the one who must rekindle the hates. Somehow, those complaints we shared made Che a visionary while they made me an executioner. He pulled the trigger with magnanimity; I pulled the trigger with a curse. And so I am left cursing at the targets we did not hit.

Once ensconced at our training camp, Che showed that he was quite a marksman. He became the protégé of our teacher, old Colonel Bayo, a distinguished Spanish Loyalist commander. From what wax museum did Bayo emerge? I can see him supervising a mock charge down a culvert, buttons polished, his monocle flashing in the Aztec light. We had to respect his advice because he had come through several wars magnificently intact. He did not seem to respect any of us, until Che came along to win the Colonel's highest marks. Che kept his rifle cleaner than he kept his syringe. He was always the professional and never the elitist, though many societies confuse these categories.

Che was also a natural healer. Healing, he could tell, was a good example of something that began as an idea and had to end as an act. Che could see that I needed his ministrations. While he had left his wife with her blessings, he had heard about my involuntary divorce and would not be kept from discussing it. In the midst of our drills, how did we find time to talk about women? Men will always find the time.

I told Che that I was ashamed of what love once meant to me.

"Of course, Jefe. Do you think we're in this line of work because we can't love? Don't believe it. Revolutionaries simply become aware that eros is a piecemeal approach to opening the walls of fear between all of us. We are driven to take more drastic measures. For men like us, there can be only one choice: revolution or heartbreak."

Put that way, I did not have much of a dilemma. Still, I wanted to take back my son.

"You must think of him as an illustrious martyr. In a revolution, a man's wife and child are the first casualties."

Che could be droll but he could also be blunt.

"Listen, we have been forced into the company of men. It is not the life we would have chosen but we are in our element here. We are unhampered, free to do what we must. We are not threatened here, except by spies and foreign operatives . . . ."

"What are you suggesting?"

"Nothing so terrible. All men have feelings of self-love. And all men suffer from homosexual flight. Even homosexuals, no? I would propose that a man's greatness may often be measured by the exalted place to which his 'flight' powers him."

Che had no need to evade the topic of this great evasion. I have been evading it for how long now, for how many twists of this tape? I won't any longer. Go ahead, Che my beloved. Like a good spouse, I will let him speak my thoughts.

"I do not oppose homosexuality because it is unnatural or bestial. Those are objections that belong to clerics, not socialists. I oppose homosexuality because it is a profound form of turning inward, a retreat toward the familiar, a collapse upon one's self."

Che could never have collapsed upon himself. He was the ultimate materialist, for whom even the spiritual was made palpable. In the Sierra Maestra, *nuestro maestro*, he would point to an underground spring and insist that the force which made the spring rise was the same force that made us revolutionaries. An historical version of gravity? It is one of those concepts I can understand but can't possibly explain. I need Guevara here to explain it.

Once he found an imperialist girlie magazine stuffed in one his unit's rucksacks. No one dared come forward to claim it. Yet Che treated the object with tolerance, not outrage. He wasn't disgusted by his discovery, he was delighted by its potential for exposing the leading edge of the conflict. He made it the number one topic on the day's forced march. Remarkably, he got the men to critique sexual objectification in the language of lumberjacks. Che was exultant but cautioned against a quick victory. He was the one to make the point that our revolution was bound to make this magazine, and so many artifacts like it, more valuable, more significant, more rare—right up until they disappeared forever.

He must return to run his poetry workshops. Only Che would have made my troops scribble. He assigned the topics: "An Ode to Expropriation," free verse. He would act as a literary jury. He gave kudos to sentries, prizes to mountain guides. Wasn't Camilo Cienfuegos, our "uncut diamond," one of Che's discoveries? He could have coaxed fluency from a piece of gypsum. He was trying to get all new recruits to express in their own way the reasons they had joined our ranks. Che would not let them be distracted by deprivation or rage from the larger, more tender implications of their soldiering.

Only he could have wept at his promotion to Major: he was always sniffling, always too moist, as if about to gush. He wanted me to think it was his hay fever, but I knew it was his humanity. Once he became an officer, he resolved that officers should eat only after all their subordinates had eaten, that he would smoke only if there was enough tobacco for everyone. Later, as foreign minister, he shunned special privileges. He went through an entire state tour of Africa without any socks because he had worn out his ration of two pairs per year. He was indeed not fond of money. He was fond of bringing salves and smallpox vaccine to the *guajiros*. When whole villages lined up, less to be immunized than to touch his khakis for good luck, Che would tell them, "I'm no messiah, I'm a doctor. The Church gave you one Christ, we will give you thousands of doctors . . . ."

Doctor Guevara's prescription was socialism. His medicine was applied with the understanding that all of us were sick.

"Man is a congenital leaner," Che would gasp, as he

himself leaned for a rest against a tree stump. "From the first moment, we are dependent, cooperative. We can't survive a day without help, encouragement or the products of some stranger's labor. This weakness is our strength. In freedom, we will all become slaves: slaves to each other. We will share and share until all we have is each other. Socialism is an admission of how much we need everyone else."

Listening to Che's impassioned seminar that went into session whenever we found a moment's safety, I would feel that resistance, that pleasantly painful sensation of running against the wind, which I have always felt when nearing the truth. But I was not a socialist yet; I was still something of a brute. It's not true that I was cleverly postponing the unveiling of my true intentions until victory. I could not have found those true intentions except through victory. For a decade, I played hide-and-seek with them. I got warmer and warmer until I burned with a clear doctrine in my grasp.

And it wasn't all Che's doing. He was not the "bad influence" that our outraged Yankee parents love to blame. There were many times in the mountains when Che would lose me utterly, especially when he lost himself in phraseology. I couldn't decode him when he swore that my greatest opponent was "concrete social reality," that my politics were "petit bourgeois nationalism in the guise of action-oriented careerist lumpenism," that "the dialectic" was validated each time a defeat made us more resolute, or that "historical materialism" was just the lens that sharpened our vision of why men have to do what they do to other men.

Like Che, I had gone to the mountains in the service of my own catchwords. The fight was for sovereignty, justice, and so on. But these were the ex-student's starting blocks, the standard justifications. A revolution, a lasting one, must brush aside all that is standard. We saw this as soon as we'd established our first liberated zone, our miniature Cuba in the muddy foothills. Once we began to live as the *campesinos* lived, we ceased fighting for abstractions. Suddenly we were fighting for a schoolhouse, for a new drainage pipe, for the treatment of glaucoma, for a way to keep the *macaguera* bugs from devouring our hides. We had obtained a real program because we had suffered real agonies, because we ourselves were hungry, were diseased, were powerless, were bitten.

I became a revolutionary by making the revolution. Anyone can. Haven't I shown how poorly prepared I was? I must have been a master improviser. When I came to streams that couldn't be forded, I built a bridge from matchsticks. Did this make me an engineer? Did it matter so long as I made it across? I remember that Che called these improbable adaptations "Fidelisms." I was profoundly touched. I recall the astonishment he felt when he found himself capable of his own. I remember his wire after an ambush in the Escambray: "Escaped by means of a dozen Fidelisms. This can't be life. It must be a movie!"

I also remember those intervals when he would sneak off to coddle himself, to collapse in his hammock and sip from the brandy reserved for the wounded. Once, he threw a cigar butt in the eye of a private who'd unwittingly interrupted Che's daily ritual of making an entry in his journal. It doesn't matter, dear warrior. Our people know all about your lapses. They forgive everything. They have a saying: "Even Che grew tired of being Che."

Do they let Fidel tire of being Fidel? They would probably be relieved if I did.

I should be pleased to invoke the memory of so many exemplary dead. Directing the people's attention toward all these mythic beings allows me to be mundane. I can get as filthy as I like, wading through today's dirty work. I can remain *el caballo*, the horse who is saddled with the possible. What a bore it is to be a saint! I don't see how Chairman Mao endured it. I submit to the "cult of personality" grudgingly, as I submit to my own personality, to that absolutist within. What vexes one should vex all; what tickles you, let it tickle me just a little. When I have a stiff neck or influenza or a bout of self-chastisement, it does me no good to be worshipped. I have tried to discourage it. I have limited the distribution of official portraits and medallions. If I've been made into something of a god, then I'm a pagan god, an animist force. I am found everywhere and nowhere—especially now, with Celia gone, with my last tie to domesticity broken. I am embodied in every hydraulic project, in the cattle-breeding program, in the smallest Committee for the Defense of the Revolution. That's fine, so long as they never catch up with this god, so long as they don't think he's residing in my aching frame.

Let them pray to Che. He's not going anywhere, he has no more amendments to make. Let them try to emulate Camilo Cienfuegos! Camilo, who began gruffly pretending he knew everything and ended more gruffly because he did. Camilo, with his cigars longer than mine, his *sombrero*, his horseface too masculine to match his openness, his admission that he was ashamed to be a Cuban, his filthy jokes and his clean laughter, his hilarious amazement at the acts he undertook, the enemy outposts he overran singlehandedly, the many times he was sick in the bushes until he learned to quell his hungers gradually, to stalk satisfaction step-by-step. Camilo's untutored incandescence was our discipline's highest expression. It was no logistical accident that I sent him ahead of me to take charge of Havana. I wanted the world to see what the guerrilla struggle had forged, what Camilo had wrought from the raw material of a simple "molasses maker." Camilo, I went to see your mother last month. As always, she kissed me wetly on the forehead. She served me her special *flan*. I ate it for you, fallen hawk. I eat for all of us.

PAUSE: TIME IS A POORLY TRAINED SERVANT

Do you hear? The cooks are stirring in their cabins. They are up at dawn to fix me my breakfast. Who am I to complain? When they see me here at the table, they'll think I've been waiting impatiently for them. I must not disappoint them. They will put on a steak, six eggs or so, to go with mangoes and yogurt. Can I really choke it all down? My capacity should not astound me. It is the capacity of a nation's empty stomach.

In every endeavor of historic magnitude, where a group of men come to act as a single organism, one man is bound to become the head, one the legs, one the broad arms, one the heart, and one, of course, becomes the mouth. At the start, I don't think any of us knew which function was meant for us. In the hills, we were innocent unspecialized apes, swinging from tree to tree. It was contact with the masses that made one of us the monkey who could kill, one the monkey who could rule, another the monkey who could explain. It is the people who required these poses from us.

"Todos a la plaza con Fidel!" When I sing my song, the people are my metronome. They provide the beat, they enforce spontaneity, and I do my best thinking when the words are at the tip of my tongue. I am a defense lawyer still, with all Cuba for a courtroom. I pride myself on memorizing the particulars of a case. I can quote last year's grapefruit production per hectare or the number of Yan-

kee battalions at Guantánamo. Responding to immediate threats, denying the most recent slanders, my words are given precision by a precise context. My ideas are mere raw material to be finished in the minds of the masses. That's what saves me from banality. After my slogans have been met with raucous approval, they flutter away like flamingos above the marsh of the crowd.

Without listeners, I have no way of telling if I am off-key. Who knows? This dictation of mine may not be an autobiography after all, but an advocate's summary plea for a life spent in strife; or the bookkeeping of a grocer taking stock of his island store; or the casualty report of a careless general; or a non-believer's impromptu last rites. Despite the heavy tread of my boots, I don't always know where I'm going. Despite the firm salute to the troops in review, I am not above doubt.

A man raises his voice or his pen or his gun. Who can say what targets he will hit?

This is a complex problem: intentions and results. We confront it continually in a new society, a self-educated society, a society where every act, however base, is justified by the noblest motives. In evaluating a housing project, or an oil painting, or this effort of mine, we must take account of deviations caused by poor craftsmanship or by discoveries made along the way. I have advanced the formula, "Within the revolution, everything. Outside the revolution, nothing." But do we make up our minds on the basis of what has been completed or on the basis of what was hoped to be completed?

In creative enterprise especially, can we even ask to know all that was intended? I am aware of the dangers of state interference in art. One of my last clients as a lawyer was the sculptor Fidalgo. For the crime of having chiseled four words from Martí, "To Cuba, which suffers . . .", at the base of a government-commissioned bust, Fidalgo's studio was ransacked by Batista's elite detachment of goons. The worst devastation was saved for Fidalgo's lifelong obsession: his castings of the hands of famous personages. I helped him sue for damages, as if restitution were possible, and though this is one of the few cases I lost, it is one of the few I remember. I can still see those shattered hands on the workshop floor, fingers turned to white shards. There is nothing so defenseless as the human hand and its works.

I am on record as stating that the enemy is imperialism, not abstract art. I am no advocate of the Russians' socialist realism, which is not at all realistic, but romantic, portraying a proletariat that is nothing but sinew and smiles. Yet I have observed a tendency among our artists to seek out the most arcane approaches. Twenty years after the avowed establishment of a popular culture, there is still a contest to create the most intricate artistic puzzles. Among our intellectuals, we still find a worship of obscurantism. Look, an obscurantist word! Our poets and painters meet after midnight to celebrate ambiguity. But art is about man and man is not a cloud of smoke. Give us the forces that shape behavior, give us the whole!

Have I given you the whole? Will my creation be deemed "within the revolution"?

According to the aesthetic of some party members, an artist gains in significance when he is incomprehensible. This bohemian clique wears their isolation like a badge, the very proof of their gifts. You'd think they would seek attention, you'd hope they would welcome serious scrutiny of their work!

But what is the point of this tirade? Maybe it has something to do with the way I've told my story. I would have liked to tell it in the manner of Hemingway, that other Ernesto in my life. As a boy, I devoured his writings. Hunting and fishing at Las Manacas, I was guided by Nick Adams, my counterpart in the cool Northern woods. *For Whom The Bell Tolls* was the one book I carried throughout the war. It contains valuable strategic precedents for the small guerrilla band.

I have been many times to inspect Hemingway's shady *finca*, with the tower where he went to write standing up so that he would write quickly. I talk standing up but that doesn't seem to restrain me. Language is very much like money and Hemingway came from the land where it is always possible to put some aside. Here we flash what little we've got. We speak the speech of spendthrifts.

But that's not the reason I have high regard for this writer. No. What makes Hemingway a great artist, honored in both the socialist and capitalist camps, is that he was not afraid of simplicity. He was a hunter of the direct. He never leaned on the crutch of metaphor—as I have just done. For Hemingway, a thing is what it is, simply and no more. His men and women reveal their character solely through action or inaction. "Pappa" certainly revealed his character when I met him, by accident, at Rancho Boyeros Airport.

"The two 'beards,' eh?" I joked, feebly. I was truly dumbfounded.

"I've been waiting for an honorary commission in your army. I guess I'm a little too old to lead men into battle. Or perhaps you had bad reports on the quality of my daiquiris . . ."

"You had only to volunteer."

"I have given my best years to Cuba. But now I am going away . . . ."

"Why?"

"I heard a nasty rumor that you are nationalizing American industry, and since I'm an American industry, I'm not sure I want to know how it feels to be nationalized . . . ."

"A writer should never become an industry."

"That's the problem. An industry always needs more raw material, more tungsten and chrome . . . ."

"Stay here. We will give you something to write about."

"I can't, it's finished. Batista's butchers shot my best hound dog . . . ."

"He was not their only victim."

"I know, Chief. But it would be obscene for me to speak of any loss except my own."

"I was informed of the incident. The man responsible was hanged."

"That was not necessary."

"A man does many things that are not necessary."

"But you don't mean the Revolution, do you?"

" 'Revolution is no opium.' " I was quoting his words back at him. " 'Revolution is a catharsis; an ecstasy that can only be prolonged by tyranny. The opiums are for before and after . . . .' "

"Bravo! . . . . I wish you luck."

"We will make a sportsman's paradise . . . ."

"Call me when it's ready. In the meantime, never trust an American congressman. Okay, Chief?"

I stayed on the tarmac and waved goodbye. Pausing before he entered the plane, Ernesto pulled a miniature Cuban flag from his safari jacket and kissed it.

"You will always be welcome!" I cried. "As long as I am here, as long as the Revolution survives . . . ."

He shouted back, "Man must not merely survive. Man must prevail!"

153

He was flying off to kill himself. They say he knew that his kind of American, the naive enthusiast, was going extinct. They say he could no longer fish or hunt the way he liked. They say he was tired of wrestling with what he feared most. Will they soon be saying these things about me?

This creeping decrepitude has no glory. Old age is one assassin even I cannot dodge. How can I "prevail" at first base?

I was moved there just yesterday. "A suggestion from the cadre," Pepin told me at the bat-rack. "For the good of the club." How could I protest? They shoved an infielder's mitt at me—it looked like a leather *tortilla*—and took away the glove that fit me so well, with the deep pocket made by so many catches. I was forced to give up the pitcher's mound, and with it the right to be at the center of every play. The right to set the *pelota* in motion. I tried not to grumble. It is imperative that I part with some of my responsibilities. It is instructional for the team to see El Jefe step aside. But first base! The initial stop on the express route to senility! From this station, you witness "the twilight of your career." That is one light I planned never to see.

The game ended mercifully. Called on account of a hurricane. Raúl's Red Sox led Fidel's *Barbudos*, 17-14. This would have been the three hundreth win for *los rojos*, while my squad has only two hundred and twelve. We've been keeping track of the series since we played those exhibitions games in the summer of '61. That was the first summer under socialism, the summer of the great harvest, the summer after we repulsed the Yankees at Playa Girón. Wasn't it also the first summer when we were forced to let the women play? They'd never been interested before but suddenly they were so insistent. Even

154

you, Celia. Remember? I showed you how to "choke up." It was a summer of great patience and a summer of hope.

My *Barbudos* are hoping still. We might have rallied to win this one had it not been for the dispute over Ramiro's double. Play was held up for half an hour while the coaches argued about whether the ball had grazed some palm leaves along the rightfield foul line. I didn't interfere. These people don't shrink from a good fight—or a bad one. Sportsmanship becomes an impossibility when each man is his own judge. It was bad enough when we were a nation of contestants. Now we're a nation of umpires.

Finally, the parties appealed to me, as I knew they would. They complained about the condition of the field. But I'm no groundskeeper, no Colonel Ruppert or George Steinbrenner. I can't invest in grandstands or a green diamond—down here, the grass always bakes brown. I told my men they were getting spoiled.

"We're lucky to have a field, to have arms and legs to play with . . . ."

What if the superpowers had seen us? What if the C.I.A. had chosen this moment to make its move? Half the Central Committee was in on the argument, stomping on the bases, kicking up all the dust they could raise.

It's true, my *compañeros* and I often act like schoolboys. It's also deceptive. Even at play, we are meditating upon survival. We are priests with pistols: our life in this place is a curious blend of the athletic and the monastic. First we read, preferably from Marx or the latest bestseller about Watergate and other Yankee scandals. Next we hunt, substituting wild grouse for our real targets. Then we shadow box, to keep trim for that last round which never comes.

When yesterday's downpour came, making our game and its rulebook irrelevant, we scooped up our rifles and left the bats to warp at home plate. We zigzagged like commandos to the main barracks' veranda. Raúl split open a melon for our midday meal. Though we all had official duties to perform, we loitered about until the storm had spent itself in the grooves of Italian tile over our wanted heads. Once more, we were an army. Once more, we had made an heroic escape: out of breath and on the run, with rain in our beards and mud in our sneakers. Once more, we could sniff one another's exertion and dampness and ardor.

Reminded of that best of times, when frustration was just another patrol we could skirt, I was nearly content. I only wish there had not been so many changes in my starting lineup. Where was my original "barnstorming" nine? If death played on our side, why didn't it take me, the captain, when I was so primed? Why do I have to be the one left to keep the game going?

Humanity's progress is ceaseless, and though it appears to move at a crawl, it is always too quick for its victims. Time is a poorly trained servant: he tries to wait at attention, linen folded over one arm, but he grows restless, sneaks off, phones his girlfriend. Tonight, this morning, I have not been an "historic figure" reciting his memoirs. I have been a referee blowing his whistle and screaming, "Time out!" But who hears me? What contest do I control? Even in *el beisbol*, the sport with no clock, there has to be a last pitch.

PAUSE: THE UNIMAGINABLE IS WHAT HAPPENS EVERY DAY

Perhaps I should take this opportunity to dictate my will. I remember the last time. I was hiding in the cushionless back seat of a Dodge sedan. It was taking me to the dock where the *Granma* was waiting to take me to my death. I used the back of a Mexican leaflet for my paper and a comrade's knee for my desk. I was my own probate. Though I anticipated imminent extinction, I could not list a legacy, I the great list maker! What was I leaving behind? Two pairs of shoes—and Fidelito. And I did not even have him! I specified only that I desired custody of the boy to be given to a childless Cuban widow who hid me when I arrived in Mexico.

I had better be careful with my dying wishes this time, since I lived to see the last one come true, or nearly come true. When the war began to turn in our favor, Mirta grew convinced that it was not safe for Fidel Castro's son to stay in Havana. She let my sister Lidia take the boy to the widow in Mexico. Unfortunately, he was not there more than a few weeks when he was kidnapped, stolen from Lidia's car at the intersection of Martí and Revolución in the town of Tacubaya. One does not forget such place names. The kidnappers turned out to be Batista agents, who may have had the idea that I would stop the whole Revolution to pay their ransom. As if I could have stopped the Revolution! Once revealed to the press, this act of barbarism, like all the others, worked against the dictatorship. Quietly, they summoned Mirta to take Fidelito home.

This was the last I would hear of him until my triumphal march into Havana. Our army had stopped for lunch at the Hatuey brewery in El Cotorro, on the outskirts of the capital. I can still hear the squealing brewery sirens welcoming me! Camilo was already in the lunchroom ahead of me but I never got to eat. A messenger arrived with word that my son was waiting for me at a nearby Shell service station. "*Vamos!*" I was at the door. My hungry troops groaned. By the time our entourage reached the station, we were mobbed with well-wishers. I couldn't find Fidelito. I was ready to shoot my rifle in the air. Then there were shouts from the tank ahead of my jeep. The gunners were holding my boy aloft—I don't know how I recognized him as my boy—passing him around like a piece of conquered booty. As usual, my men couldn't know how much truth was contained in their instinctive gesture. Fidelito reached me like a piece of driftwood floating on waves of green fatigues. Someone had dressed Fidelito in a midget-sized uniform. I never got to ask him who it was. I know it wasn't his mother. Then I was reaching into the gyrating octopus that was my honor guard, cleaving the converging diagonals of upraised weapons until I could take the boy from Camilo, could assess the bulk of my progeny, could grasp the miracle bred from my youthful error, could hug him. My jeep started violently and he hung onto me as Mirta once had.

Fidelito rode at my side all the way to Havana. I would like to say that this plump little boy did not mean anything special to me after all the starving little boys I had seen. I would like to say that this token of my victory over Mirta did not make my larger victory more sweet. I would like to say that this victory was lasting, that my son still rides by my side.

Couldn't he see that I had given him a revolution? Wasn't that enough? Why does it end in wrangling each time we meet? Celia, you tried your best to make me see his side. Alright, I understand that Fidelito was brought along amidst turbulent conditions. *Claro*. But were they any more turbulent than the conditions withstood by those *guajiro* children who must scavenge their way to adulthood one meal at a time? I know, too, that I cast a great shadow. It's a fine excuse but my son cannot live his life with excuses for company.

Didn't I get him a scholarship to Moscow University for advanced studies in color theory, medieval ikons, folk art, any subject that caught his overtrained eye? But Moscow, it seems, was still not far enough away from me.

Since I've done everything, Fidelito does nothing. Oh, one thing. He beats me at ping-pong. He appears to enjoy that. He's as tall as I am but you'd never know it. He holds himself so sheepishly. In him, there is displayed my own weakness for long hours at the dining table, for sweets and useless speculation, which I have trained out, marched out, willed away. My son moves in slow motion. He revels in a sorrowful compassion for everything and everyone. He practically throbs with pity, the same pity that prompts me to act. But he never acts. His benevolence makes me squirm.

I don't like his friends either. They are a little too "artistic," and so is my boy. I fear the true cause of his bachelorhood. But then I am a bachelor too. Still, some reasons are reasonable, some unspeakable. If he is a painter, where are his paintings? I have seen only napkin art. The patience I've shown my son has been greater than the patience I reserve for our society's most backward sectors. If he cannot contribute, he will go to a camp.

This time I won't bequeath my son the least concern. He wouldn't take it anyway. This time I will not think only of lineage. I know now that the members of my family are the millions and millions of forward-looking people everywhere. I have brothers in Angola, sisters in Zimbabwe, children in Kuwait. The only true family is the family in arms. And I care no more for my blood relations—be it resentful Fidelito, spiteful Juana, or inspirational Raúl—than I do for my diplomatic relations. Truly, I care about them less. I have said goodbye, as all men must, to mother and sister and cousin, as we must one day say goodbye to our prized playthings and our esteemed pets and our treasured automobiles and our cherished tastes and our precious lusts and our chosen theories. The prospect of death dampens all grasping, cures all private fetishes. And the revolutionary must adhere to the perspective of death in life. So long, *hasta luego!* Stop grabbing and you will get everything.

No paltry clan will grieve for me, or gather around my executor, eager to get their hands on my estate. My estate is the state. I will be survived by a whole people.

Let the people enjoy my death, since their enemies will. Let them turn my memorial to sport. Why not? A good contest is what the Cubans crave, and I am one of them. I will bury this tape outside Santa Clara, on the grounds of a model citrus farm, under the arthritic tendrils of the district's tallest *ceiba* tree. I won't tell anyone. I'll leave clues at all the ministries, on the scoreboards, in the ice cream cones at *La Coppelia*. I'll make the nation hunt for its inheritance, for this final sermon. Anti-social elements will not be eligible for the grand prize. And what will that finder's fee be? An insignia of merit in the form of Che's red star, fifty pounds of sugar, a lifetime supply of hardballs, and the equivalent in gold bullion of all foreign exchange I have puffed away all these years with my taste for export-quality *Montecristo A's!* A huff and a puff: that is all this tyrant has hoarded.

"I, Fidel Castro Ruz, a/k/a Alejandro, being of sound, unrevisionist mind and flabby, unscathed body . . . ."

To Mamma and Pappa, I leave one share in the United Fruit Company, Cuban Division.

To sister Juana, I leave a combination cigarette lighter and molotov cocktail.

To sister Lidia, this retreat and all its grounds, to be used as a child care center.

To brother Raúl, my best rifle, my harpoon, my podium.

To son Fidelito, a world without me in it.

To wife Mirta, a drop of jism.

To friend Celia, posthumously, an academy for day-dreamers.

To the fisherman Pérez, more posthumously, I leave one Soviet trawler in good working order—if one can be found!

To Batista, a second hand condom and a Coppertone tan.

To Kennedy and Khrushchev, one missile each up the wrong end.

To Nixon and Brezhnev, my unused Gillette.

To Uncle Ho and Chairman Mao, my solidarity stuffed in a sack of fertilizer.

To Luis Tiant, a humidor. And to whom will I leave the thermidor?

To the peasants, museums. To the prostitutes, pick-axes. To the poets, walkie-talkies.

To Cuba, I offer the results of my amateur garden-ing—twenty *arrobas* of hybrid tomatoes—along with a gardener's warning: one season of neglect and the weeds start returning.

To Latin America, I leave slogans in the mouths of your children when I would rather leave bread.

To Che and Camilo and Abel and Inti and Allende and all the heroic Chicos, a trail map of paradise.

To the *Estados Unidos*, hated lover, worthy foe, tyrant and tease, I leave the exclusive television rights to my entombment. This must take place at the first American-Cuban World Series in Anti-Yankee Stadium. The proceed-ings will start with my videotaped rendition of Lou Gehrig's farewell—"I am the luckiest man in the world," flashed across the scoreboard—and end with my final cry of *"Patria o Muerte!"* That cry will be echoed by ten thousand cheerleaders from small towns in East Texas. The *gusanos* in the bleachers will fling their caps high. The "freedom flotilla" will sweep the infield with their tongues. A Marine Honor Guard will present the Cuban colors, which are also red, white and blue. Billy Graham will lead the benediction. Régis Debray will throw out the first ball. Pat Boone and the Grupo Moncada will sing a medley of "The International" and "The Ballad of the Green Berets." Desi Arnaz and Pérez Prado will lead the Notre Dame Marching Band. J. Edgar Hoover will peddle hot dogs. Miss Barbara Walters will do the play-by-play. In a warmup bout, Kid Gavilan will outpoint Joe Louis. The C.I.A.'s Havana bureau chiefs, led by Meyer Lansky, will challenge the Venceremos Brigade in an Old-Timers Game; Mickey Mantle will lose an arm-wrestling match to the ghost of Roberto Clemente; the Commissioner will okay a deal giving Puerto Rico back to the Puerto Ricans for a country-to-be-named-later. Our hemisphere of corn and yucca, of cowboys and slaves, will finally be at peace.

Ay, Fidel! Enough dreaming! Now I know that fatigue has found me. I am dreaming with my eyes open.

A revolution gives priority to dreams. The moment of victory is a moment of pure chaos—like the chaos of nature, the hidden structure of the forest, the unconscious. Beautiful new imagery rises into view. The usual resistance has been cast away; the obstacles to free association have been blown up with mortars. Camilo Cienfuegos releasing the doves in the Presidential Palace because "they, too, have a right to freedom." Did this happen or did I merely want it to happen? The rehabilitation of Havana's prostitutes with the therapy of pure love. Why not? The elimination of polio and illiteracy and colonial mentality, all in one decade. If we can do the impossible while asleep then why not when awake? In such heady situations, the oppressed and their oppressed imaginations explode with civic works born from an inner architecture, from the *plazas* that grace the chambers of the heart.

But soon the liberators must put their liberated dreams in a drawer. They must recognize their utopianism as an efficient intoxicant, distracting the masses from tackling the tasks of the present. Before we can have what no men ever had—thus sticking our necks into a new noose—we must have what all men ought to have. We want decent housing and medical care, increased educational levels, a secure and peaceful society with honest goals, an open and forthright public debate, lively cultural expression, respect for one another and our various races, a place to go dancing on Saturday night and of course, free baseball games.

And we've nearly got it! In Cuba today we have made the necessary transition from dream time, to borrow a phrase from our aboriginal brothers, to work time. Yet while we better ourselves economically, we must never lose that capacity to dream. While we concentrate on the upgrading of real conditions, there must be no end to unreal visions. The spiritual goals of our struggle must be kept alive. This is the great irony for all materialists. This is what makes me and my staff chuckle over an all-night session of dominoes. We insist that man is a creature of concrete needs, that the wants of the stomach must be satisfied before we can consider the wants of the soul; yet we place our regime in jeopardy when we instill in our people the illusion that they will be happy with more pounds of pork per week, larger apartments, perhaps a Ford or Volga someday. Strangely enough, we can't compete in this arena with the anti-materialists. We've accomplished what is hard but not what is easy.

We give the people self-esteem, they want electric can

openers. We give them parks with floating ampitheatres, they want mayonnaise. We give them monuments, they want discos. We give them institutes for the appreciation of every aspect of their common heritage, they want blue jeans. Let them have it. "Let my people go . . . ."

Socialism cannot afford these desires—they burst our budgets, both fiscal and psychic. We can put fifty thousand more miles on the imperialists' outworn cars but we don't want to ride on their outworn ideas as well. If human beings can be bought off by anything, the Yankees will buy them. Our cry is that the Cuban masses must continue to fashion demands for themselves that cannot be satisfied by any known economy or realm.

I know that solidarity is a terrible burden. I know too, that a pond can't be cleaned without stirring up a little mud. All the grumbling inspires me. The defections assure me that we remain faithful to our creed of freedom through sacrifice.

This freedom is not a guarantee found in a constitution scrawled on parchment. This freedom is not merely free choice, since there is no choice before the historical imperative. It is not free speech, since all genuine dissent must end in the pointing of weapons. And yet I have need of this word: freedom. It is the next generation—the ones we are making literate, the ones who are born with Marx, the ones who will have a socialist movement without excuses, with power—that will define what I've been seeking.

In the meantime, we are working to make the most private fantasies public domain. Hand them over! Let's all share! No wonder I get into trouble when I get into bed. My dreams have become practical matters—I don't need the darkness to find them. One immense pool of yearnings will be feeding my reveries long after sleep defeats me for good.

The night Celia died, I dreamed about a stolid peasant girl, an implacable she-ox moving with deliberation down a road of light. She had hooved feet but the prettiest silver bracelet flopping 'round her ankle. When I approached, in the form of a mischievous breeze at her back, the woman turned to clay. When I touched her with my invisible hands, the clay melted, water ran down her back from the spigots of my fingers. When I stooped to rescue her bracelet from this sudden decay, I was driven to my knees by an avalanche of light. Nearly blinded, I looked up and saw the peasant girl's legs sprouting needles of hair. The hair turned to wobbly black knives aimed at my eyes.

If I could just turn out the light and dream about Cuba! Cuba, our congenial life raft, our natural beauty reclining on her Caribbean couch. This spine of a slumbering green alligator, this swamp of desires, this trampoline of wills, this laboratory of nuance. Coooo-ba: to this day, nobody knows what it means.

Is this the same realm I imagined night after night as I lay awake in the mountains, peering down from my pine needle perch? Can I conjure up the lure that destination once held for me? Do I dare? There, down there, shrouded in steam and perpetual sun, was the Cuba I was about to claim, a Cuba prepared to salute the flag of Castro. And who was this Castro kid? A loyal son or a scourge? When I shot my rounds, I had no idea that each cartridge shell was a seed, that every bullet would blossom into a polyclinic, a sports palace, a secondary school. The Cuba I wanted to conquer was a country without housing shortages, without trade deficits, without Russian advisors, without rehabilitation centers, without refugees, without upstart poets, without women's consciousness groups, without bureaucracies, without government. My Cuba was a void, as clean a place as I have always been dirty, as or-

165

derly as I have always been messy. I would empty the trash-bins called cities. I would evacuate everything humdrum. My Cuba was to be one unattended playground, where the edifice of commerce had fallen like a stage set along with the grim impositions of habit. This nation would survive on its nerve, would barter presumption, a currency more solid than gold. Debts would be settled on the spot, including debts of love, with no delays for grudges or revenge. Work wouldn't be mandatory or compensatory, but exquisite craft, an homage to our hands. Culture would be a wine-press for sincerity. All music would stop, on the beat, as would flattery and fawning. False laughter, like false words, would be unthinkable in my Cuba.

But that republic I hoped to rule was the delirium of a leader's lonely fever, lacking in one binding element: the people. The widows in black shawls, the bachelors in black sunglasses, the tour guides, the bible salesmen, the second-rate plumbers and the first-rate panderers, the *macheteros* with calloused thumbs and calloused hearts, their sons who wanted to be boxers, their sons who wanted to be monks and worshipped virgins in Loretta Young movies and went with whores and mortgaged their futures for a mule. And others who were Jehovah's Witnesses and others who consulted the sea shells, and others who consulted rum and others who were going to be so happy once they got to Paris, and others who needed more time to think it over and others who were stalwart but mute and still more others, always forever and unjustifiably more others, dizzying, malingering, compliant yet thorny, who conducted their business entirely in the present tense, who besmirched the red bandana simply because it was besmirchable, and others who lived under rocks, who feared the open sky.

I could not have my Cuba any more than the Yankees could have theirs. Both fell at the same instant: mine toppled by innocence, theirs toppled by corruption; both brought down, or up, by the common life that could not help existing. "The eternal Cuba, and the fleeting Fidel . . ." Victory interrupted my dreaming and I sleepwalked toward compromise. Yes, I am finally ready for bed, but now it is morning! And with morning comes compromise, the greatest gift history can bestow. For it is only when we know what we will settle for that we find what we were after all along.

Luckily, nothing turns out the way you plan it, not even five-year-plans. The unimaginable is right before us, is what happens every day.

To get at the truth, you must be a *guerrillero*. Sneak up quietly, plan your ambush. Trust in unforeseen outcomes.

In my life, what has been most unforeseen and unimaginable is that I still have a life at all. The greatest surprise is that there are no more surprises. Remarkably, I am a settled, stable man. I run a stable government. Having thrived on the unexpected, having found my best advantage in what I could not control, this stability makes me feel forever embattled.

In this final campaign, all nights are the same, all days the same. There is a deceptive monotony to power. There is a troubling constancy to the approval that envelops me. Some mens' lives begin simply and end in complication. Mine began in complication and will end simply. He who gives orders must learn to take orders. "Give us a speech." "Go to first base." "Eat your mangoes."

Listen how the cooks are calling! How insistent they are that I be fed! That I continue! For their sake, I'll pretend to have slept. I'll revive myself with a *buchito* and the morning's diplomatic cables. The pines will be my smelling salts.

I would rather hear you calling, Celia. I would rather hand this cassette over to you for transcription or erasure. Could it be that I, who possess a nation's fellowship, no, a nation's tenderness, should now feel the lack of a singular endorsement, of contact, however indirect, with your specific grace? Why is it I must picture your crooked smile with its hint of fangs, and that hooked Galician nose, your serious olive cheeks, your collarbone showing at the opening of a grey tunic, those white strands running like urgent messages through your ebony curls? I must not omit your clarity, your silence, your restful lack of obsession. Do you mind that it's taken so many hours for your Alejandro to admit that I miss you? I don't know whether to take this admission as a victory or defeat.

The facade of the body has fallen away from me. I have trained myself too well to resist all forms of slavery, including a slavery to the senses. I have turned away from the demands of the flesh because the flesh is a first roadblock, our primary limitation. I would hope that I can become another Gandhi—well, a Latin Gandhi, soiled with blood and rum—but a Mahatma nonetheless. Of all the means at my disposal to prove I am a man, the means of desire now strikes me as the least efficient.

Tomorrow, I return to Havana and the tasks that attest to my humanity. I can't accomplish this in my office, with all those memoranda and charts. I must hop in my jeep. I must take our regime to the street. Another carton of *Montecristos*, another tin of hard candies and a pistol go in the glove compartment. The boys complain about my driving. They say I talk too much and look at the road too little. I pound the accelerator. My boots slip off the clutch. But I've yet to have an accident, and if I did I would be held accountable. I am simply one Cuban among nine million, one man among many.

I may drop in on a new factory here, a nursery there—the more unexpected my arrival, the more faith I have in what I observe. If I'm hungry, I'll try some new pizzeria favored by my aides. If I want to scrutinize Cuban cinema, I'll go to a movie house. If I need to greet the masses, I'll walk the boulevards. This has never been a matter of showing our cause has popular support. Despite those who weaken, despite the attrition in our ranks, this support has not required proof. In the cities or the canefields, I must have those imploring eyes seeking mine out. I must feel the "support of the skin" which my people give me just as well as you did, Chelita.

I must hear out every complaint. "What happened to the consignment of stoves? Where are the ball-bearings? Have we run out of coffee already? Fidel, when do we get some fresh meat?" I must be alert to every new difficulty. "Who laid these sewer lines? Where is your irrigation? Are there enough technicians? Enough *trompetas* in the band? And how is the television reception in this area? And who wants to have his book published? Who wants to blockade us? And why don't the workers come to see your exhibit? And why did your son run away?" I can only go on asking and being asked.

This exchange is the source of my strength. These demands are my salvation. Just when I think I'm snug and invulnerable, when I've settled nicely into my lonely superiority, a young girl with one eye milked-over laughs so that I can hear her rueful forgiveness of everyone, or a dying *guajiro* tugs at my sleeve with the power of a tractor, and all at once, I am caught. I am caring again.

I must remember the lesson of the fisherman Pérez: other men are all that oppress me, other men are all that can set me free.

Why so many "musts" in a man's life? Just think how

169

many years these "musts" chew up and discard! I must eat when I'm served, also when I'm not. I must be careful not to eat too much. And I must have another sustenance, a food sown from the minds of men and harvested from thin air. I must lie down and dream, if only for a few moments. I must scratch when I itch, though never while on the reviewing stand. I must clear my throat and clear the palate of my thoughts with more coffee, more tobacco. I must go to the beach and take the sedative of the waves.

Our creator, if we had one, was no state planner, sworn to efficiency: I must do so many things I do not wish to do in order to do the things I want to do. I must keep tidy. (Throw the cigar butts anywhere you like, *chico*.) I must have my soft khakis starched and pressed so that those who see me will be made comfortable. I must say a kind word to this delegation or that worthy committee. I must smile after a joke, applaud at the end of every performance, no matter how "folkloric." I must let my brothers know they are my brothers. Even if it takes a wink, that is too much time wasted!

If friends are sincere, why must they be so demanding? Sincere enemies require even more attention. For the sake of both, I must act. Then I must justify those acts. I must never answer their inquiries with the phrase, "I don't know," though no one, especially a Marxist, should ever be afraid to say he doesn't know. I must not rule in the name of ambiguity. I must not raise a banner with no words on it. I must walk confidently into my next mistake. I must draw lessons for my national classroom. I must reserve some dazzling contradiction for an encore. I must stop this harangue, I must never stop. I must survive, I must "wither away." I must deny my historic role in order to accept it. I must lead the cheers as I lay a wreath on the tomb of our times.

Look over there at Guardian! *Hola!* Nothing can wake him. My dog's curled up so safely. An hour from now, I will catch him skittering under car wheels, chasing sparrows and wisps of air. Like him, I must be true to my nature's intent. I must go forward, risking everything.

But a revolution is not just a matter of "musts." A revolution is made up of "mights" that are turned into "cans." I must keep this truth in mind, then open my mind for more truths the way I keep open a flap of my tent. I must break camp in the middle of the night. I must endure caution. I must suffer stalemate. I must be consoled by each new day in which to conspire, by one more crooked nail driven, by another mile logged, by the wind through my fingers on an empty highway. I must belong, and having belonged, I must escape. I must dive deeper, swing harder: to rule in the name of an ultimate consummation, I must know contentment, however trivial, however swift. I must finally lose myself. I must . . .